WHAT AWAITS IN THE DARK

CONTENTS

To my parents for supporting me throughout my writing career

To Petals, the family rottweiler, for being an cute lump and always proving me that looks can be deceiving (as she's about as scary as a snuggle blanket)

To Sam, my editor for going through this and surviving! (Sorry I didn't tell you how horrific it actually was)

SARAH ELLIOT

WHAT AWAITS IN THE DARK

FREAK HOUSE

The door to the attraction closed with an eerie creak, the type that would only exist in a horror story.

Antoni scoffed and rolled his eyes, wondering how many of the others were already unnerved by the simplistic sound effect. The room he was in looked to be the standard haunted house affair; a rustic, abandoned, old mansion with some supposedly creepy story about the family disappearing. The floor was dirty and the wallpaper was peeling off the walls. Dust and cobwebs were everywhere and sections of missing tiles or ominous holes spoke of neglect. The same old, boring setup that gave most normal people the idea that something terrible was lurking in the corners to come at them.

Glancing to the left, Antoni smirked almost gleefully when he found a mirror that slightly warped his appearance. He was five foot ten but always stated that he was six feet, with a handsome face that would have easily won 'The Most Handsome Face' competition anywhere he would have cared to enter. He worked out, kept his hair neat and tidy, and had a pair of sorrowful, alluring, brown eyes. He always made sure to use them to his advantage which, along with a pleasing facial structure, matched most females' idea of a perfect man. Well, the ones who were not tainted of course. He always preferred those sweet, naïve, little princesses that he could guide and protect in his own way.

Brushing off some imaginary lint from his suit jacket, Antoni set off in a random direction to try and find his hapless colleagues. They had decided that the team building exercise that they wanted to do was this haunted house attraction in town that was getting rave reviews. Initially he had had zero interest in going anywhere near the place. It was not his style and so overhyped for what it was. That was until there was the mention of Elora attending. The man had changed his opinion almost immediately and said that he would attend without question, even offering to carpool with a few of his colleagues to divert any suspicion.

Of course there was the question of inviting partners, spouses and family which the boss allowed under the condition that they paid for themselves. It made sense, as he was bringing his eldest daughter to the event, and it would be unfair for anyone else to not be allowed to bring their significant other.

When asked, Antoni said that his last partner had gone off on a backpacking trip around Europe and had called everything off. It staved off most and those who were curious would have trouble finding any further information as all her social media accounts were set to private, and she had never accepted anyone whom she did not know. It also meant that Antoni was free to pursue new conquests, though he did not mention to anyone that he had his eyes firmly set on Elora.

Too much was made about older men dating younger girls. Antoni just preferred his partners to not be corrupted by the evil of boys who did not know how to treat their princesses like they deserved. But many people took that completely the wrong way, so he did not bring it up anymore.

He heard someone shout his name which led him to his colleagues. He followed the sound to a staged room made to look like a kitchen. There were the usual pots and pans that were filled with nasty things, as well as a creepy looking basement door which would lead to one of the two potential last zones that they had to explore. Because of course, there would be a monster trying to eat them in the basement or an old witch up in the attic who would come to claim their souls or whatever the plotline was. Antoni had been busy sending messages to some potential interests in case Elora was off the market, but with how overprotective her father could be Antoni very much doubted that he would have to worry about that. She would be desperate to have some fun tonight.

Overprotective fathers always created the best princesses he had found. So easy to mould.

In the kitchen were three of his colleagues, Bryan, Sam, and Greg. Bryan and Greg were two upcoming interns who had the confidence to do pretty well for themselves but with only a single brain cell that was unfortunately shared between the pair of them. Sam was a pretty, if rather plain, secretary from the third floor who was good at making tea but not that easy on the eyes anymore. It appeared that Greg had opened the fridge which contained several packages of meat that were definitely not the types that could be purchased in the supermarkets. Suddenly, something jumped out at Bryan causing him to squeal like a child. Sam was laughing loudly at the pair, before shaking her head. "Don't think the key will be there."

"I bloody hope not," Greg said, closing the door with a distinct thump. "Fuck, sorry about that mate."

"Warn me next time!" Bryan complained, cautiously coming out from the corner he had hidden around and noticed Antoni with a start. "Oh, hi, Antoni. Thought you weren't coming?"

"I carpooled with Terry and Jade," Antoni said dismissively. "They can never keep time outside of work. What are you doing in here?"

Sam smiled. "Trying to find the key for the locks on the doors over by the stairs. The first clue we got was to obtain the book of truths from the upstairs library. Maddie figured that out by herself. Of course, we need three separate keys, so we split into teams to try and find them. We just got in here about five minutes ago before a spider jumped out at Bryan."

"It was fucking huge!" Bryan put on a scowl. "And I wasn't expecting it."

"Whatever dude," Greg replied, already busy searching through the cupboards. "Let's just try and find this key, cause we're losing time."

Antoni blinked, looking at the pair quizzically which made Sam chuckle. "It's an escape room too, so you have to complete everything in a certain time or else the Collector will come after you."

"The Collector?" Antoni asked, not moving to help as the other two started scrabbling about in the cupboards.

Sam nodded, checking through multiple drawers as she spoke. "Weren't you paying attention to the story?"

"Not really," Antoni replied, already bored with this premise. "It's just the usual routine of these places. Family goes missing. Suspected killer is still in the house. Yada yada."

Sam looked up, looking a bit bemused, but shook her head. "Oh no, this one isn't like that. See, apparently the Collector comes for those who have their names marked down for collection by the unseen forces of the universe and since we signed up, our names are all in the book. If you're innocent you can escape by finding the clues, unlocking the doors, and freeing the trapped spirits within the house, but if you're guilty you'll be caught and dragged down to Hell."

"So, we need to work out the clues, and quickly." Bryan continued.

Antoni sighed, thinking this to be a very stupid setup. "And let me guess, the Collector comes running through the house on a set timer?"

"We don't know," Greg replied. "They just said to look out for the Collector but gave no description. Creepy, eh?"

Instead of answering, Antoni turned and walked away thinking that this was all going to be a waste of time. Clearly he wasn't going to get anywhere close to Elora to act as her protector. He was going to head for the exit when he realised that they hadn't been told where the exit was. He let out a sigh of frustration. His dark eyes landed on the lock system that they had to find the keys for, and he made his way towards it, staring at the strange shapes that were required. This was going to be far harder than anyone had let on and he would be forced to deal with his unsightly colleagues for the entire time.

A movement over to his right caught his eye and he turned sharply towards it, finding himself facing a large painting of an old, withered tree with an old-fashioned swing suspended from one of the branches. On the swing was what appeared to be a young girl, wearing a long-sleeved Cinderella style dress in a goldish white, with layers of smocking all the way down to the ground. Nordic-white hair hung down almost to the ground, slightly curled in cascading river patterns that held just the smallest hints of silver and purple to them. Her facial features were covered by a black cat-mask with gold emphasis around the eyes and ears that served to give her an alluring and mysterious air. Held within her pale hands was a deep red, leather-bound book which shut with a snap as he watched.

The image moved, the girl standing up from the swing and moving towards Antoni in an eerily silent manner, seeming to become larger as she approached. Pausing just inside of the frame itself, the cat-faced girl seemed to regard him for a few moments before letting out a soft, gentle smile. "Don't follow the light if you wish to survive, Antoni..." The voice was ancient, hollow, and filled the man's heart with concern. "Though you've been on my list since the first. I will have fun collecting you."

Blinking rapidly, Antoni stared back at the portrait of the tree with the girl sitting back on the swing merely observing her book. He let out a long blowing breath, shaking his head. "Should not have filled in that stupid form. Good one though, almost got me going." Dismissing the incident, he glanced back down at the lock and saw that it had two keys already in it which confused him a little, but he then heard a sound of a delicate yelp and hurried to help.

Elora was sitting on the floor, her dainty, little hand covering her heart. Her eyes were full of tears that looked like they were about to spill forth from her large, innocent, green eyes. "Are you okay?" Antoni asked in his most soothing voice, kneeling close to the girl but not touching just yet. Even though it was so tempting to just pick her up all bridal-style and carry her around like the trophy that she would undoubtedly become.

The girl turned her attention fully upon him, looking confused for a few seconds as if she did not recognise him but then letting out a slight sigh of relief. "Oh, hello again."

For a moment Antoni forgot how to breathe as he could only stare at the perfect, little princess in front of him. Slender body, long legs covered with a pair of dark blue jeans that had a small rip in the knees. These were accompanied by a long sleeved top with a series of white bands going around the arms and a graphic of some demonic looking radio person which fit the mood of the season. Her black hair was tied back in a loose ponytail and she had gone for a bewitching fairy look for her makeup in shimmering purples and greens that just looked radiantly beautiful. Antoni would have preferred her in a sweetheart dress in a shade of white or yellow with little ballet shoes and glistening fairy wings, but he allowed that the weather wasn't exactly appropriate for that style. Though he did have to appreciate her silhouette as it was clear that she was a fine, young woman.

He'd have to take her soon or else she would be past the point of perfection.

Antoni smiled. "Are you okay, Elora?"

"Yes, sorry, I got spooked by something around the corner," Elora said with an embarrassed smile. "I guess I stumbled backwards and just sort of landed here."

That made Antoni concerned. "Are you hurt anywhere?"

"Only my pride," Elora replied, shaking her head before starting to stand up.

"Oh here, let me help you," Antoni said, immediately putting his hands underneath her armpits and lifting her upwards which pulled the cutest little surprised gasp (a startled yelp) past those soft pink lips.

Elora stared at Antoni, her delicate little fingers resting lightly on top of his big manly arms that, in Antoni's head, were clearly being appreciated, before she asked softly, "Could you let me down please?"

"Oh sorry," Antoni replied, setting her onto her feet and not noticing the way that she immediately pulled her arms into her body to hide herself away from him. "I guess I just don't know my own strength."

The girl stared at him with her large, green eyes. Antoni felt he could see several conflicting emotions in them but he knew that this was just part of the game. All the little princesses he had ever been with had little to no real interaction with proper gentlemen and rarely knew how to react to them. None of them ever took long to learn and came to appreciate his strength and abilities to be the only man in their lives that would protect them. He just had to have a little patience because this was only their second proper meeting, and it wouldn't be long until she worshipped the ground that he walked on.

That is, if her father would let her out of his sight for a moment. The thought made Antoni curious. "Where is your father?"

"Oh, he let me go in first with Clive," Elora replied. "He's coming in last to make sure that everyone who is meant to be here got here."

"I didn't see him at the entrance?" Antoni said, now a little confused as his boss was a very difficult man to miss at the best of times.

Elora blinked. "You must have, he didn't let anyone in who wasn't on his booking form. You know what he's like."

For a few seconds Antoni pondered this. His boss was that pedantic and judgemental, but he swore that he did not see him at the entrance to the attraction. He had turned up in his car, with Terry and Jade and they had stood in the queue, given the ticket confirmation to the person behind the counter and then had stepped in. Though now he thought about it, the girl at the booth had been a little strange, all dressed up in a white dress with a black cat-mask on and long, white hair cascading down to the floor. He hadn't paid attention to what she had said when he had entered the place thinking that it was just a usual spooky message to get everyone in on the premise, but now the words crept back up towards him with a very cold shudder. "One wrong step, and you'll belong to the Collector."

Shaking his head to dismiss the weirdness, Antoni snorted. "Well, I must have missed him. Let's go and find him and see if we can't find these keys to get to whatever the heck the next place is all-"

Suddenly, out of the darkness, a figure in a long, blood-stained dress lunged towards Antoni with a shriek, a sharp-tipped dagger reaching out towards him. The soulless, grey eyes swirled with black and red, and a long wailing scream piercing through the air that was a clear cry of his name.

Antoni stepped back just as the mannequin reached the end of its tether, the plastic blade just missing the air where he had stood before. It stuttered a couple of times and then chattered soundlessly before being pulled back into the cupboard where it would leap out again the next time someone strolled by. Looking down at the ground, the man who claimed to always be taller than he was saw a slightly raised section of the floor that was clearly the trigger for the phantom. He bent down to make a clear indicator with the dust around it. "We'll have to tell the others about that little jump scare when we come across them."

Elora giggled a little. "I got so startled by that thing. It was a good little trick though."

"Hmm, indeed," Antoni replied, before skirting around the floorboard to head to what appeared to be some kind of reading room where he was sure that he could hear voices.

"Though you're so brave, you didn't even flinch when that thing came towards you," Elora said as she followed him carefully. "I just nearly passed out over it, and you were just standing there like it was nothing. Which is so cool."

The praise was appreciated, even if it was not worded as Antoni would have liked. But it was a start. "I just have more world experience than you. I'm sure there'll be more jump scares awaiting us. Now, what things could possibly spook us in a library?"

"A table filled with strange renditions of your ex-girlfriends?" Elora suggested, giggling oh so innocently at her slightly twisted joke which made Antoni roll his eyes. If he were to get her into his clutches, that little bit of sassiness would have to go. Princesses should always be sweet and complimentary to their princes and never have a bad word to say about them or their pasts. It was not an acceptable thing in his eyes, but he had to remind himself that she had not been moulded yet.

Plus, her father, whilst protective, did certainly like to let her think she had a bit of freedom and explore the world, which was a bit on the silly side as she should be protected from all the dangers that could befall her. The new age ideas of how a girl should be, how females were meant to be equal to males and all that quirkiness which seemed to be polluting the airwaves these days. He wanted nothing more than to quell all that nonsense, all those pathetic wimpy males that let the females boss them about and make them do their bidding really needed a firm kick from an *Alpha* male.

These were thoughts that he mainly kept to himself, because people got way too easily offended. There was never a chance to correct them properly because it would just be turned into petty drama that only made sense to the weakest beings on the planet.

However, he was still trying to woo Elora into being his perfect princess so he would have to humour her little deviation. It wasn't much of a one either, just a little rebellion that would be easily quashed when the next mechanism or effect leapt out from behind a bookcase and made her willingly jump into his arms to be protected. So, he chuckled, "I doubt that, plus I am not the man to have that many ex-girlfriends."

"Oh really? I heard rumours that you have a plethora of exes," Elora teased back with a smug little grin.

"Who told you that?" Antoni asked, sure that office gossip never centred around his affairs of the past as none of his colleagues knew about them.

"Just someone," Elora said, stepping around to push the door to the library open. "Come on, let's get to the others, huh?"

A feeling of trepidation fell over Antoni, though he couldn't quite place why. He wasn't getting creeped out by this place, there was nothing in here that could hurt him in any way. It was just a scary attraction. The most danger he would be in would be from tripping over something as he ran away with the others. But there was a look in Elora's eyes now that made him feel distinctively uneasy and he could not put a finger on it. Sure, she was bright and sharp-witted, but her mentioning him having many exes but not saying who had told her just made him wonder.

He turned his head back towards the painting with the girl on the swing, recalling her strange, monotone words. He found that the swing was empty save for a slight swaying that was caused by the wind blowing it. "Are you sure that you don't want to check out somewhere else first?" he asked, as he turned back to Elora, his words feeling thick and heavy on his tongue. "I mean the others seemed to think…"

"Scared of some books, are you Antoni?" Elora asked, a teasing grin on her face. "Or is it the notion of what you may find if you look a little too far into yourself?"

For the briefest of seconds, Antoni thought that he saw Elora change into a small red skinned creature with dainty, cloven feet, a long, pointed tail and sharp, black horns that were laced with white bands around them. Deep yellow eyes stared unblinkingly at him with a wicked smirk crossing a beautiful mouth that was filled with razor sharp teeth.

A series of quick blinks brought the pretty young girl back into his vision and Antoni rubbed at his head before he let out a breath. "What the hell?"

"Are you okay, Antoni?" Elora said in the sweetest voice, peering up at him with her beautiful, green eyes that were full of nothing but peace and innocence. Immediately Antoni felt himself relax.

He nodded as he gave her a stupidly wide smile. "Yes, perfectly. Sorry, I took a little turn for a moment there, I must be dehydrated. Shall we go and explore the spooky library and see if we can find a key?"

"Yes, though you'll have to protect me from all the horrible ghosts in there," Elora replied, latching onto his arm with a delicate, little grip that had Antoni's pride purring with delight.

He puffed out his chest and started to lead the way into the room, feeling like the cat who had got all the cream. Briefly, his eyes were drawn to a small, square portrait by the door which showed the white-haired girl from before, still adorned in the black and gold cat-mask. She seemed to stare at him unflinchingly before raising a single finger into the air to slowly wag it at him. Scoffing, he opted to ignore the strange being and headed into the library, certain that he was going to outsmart whatever creepy encounter that could be brought up here.

The moment he stepped through the doors, an immense feeling of cold plunged straight into Antoni's body, virtually robbing him of all the heat that he had. Immediately he wrapped his arms around himself. He could not control his chattering teeth nor the goosebumps appearing all over his arms and rushing horribly over his neck.

He stared around the shelves, finding them covered in icicles that looked as sharp as knives. They glinted in a strange, blue firelight that was coming from somewhere deeper into the room. There were huge, black candles that Antoni knew were impossible, but his eyes were not deceiving him. Shaking his head, he turned to look for Elora and saw that the girl was just standing around, as if nothing strange were going on, standing on her tiptoes while running her fingers along the spines of a very high shelf.

"Elora?" he managed to stammer out, his breath fogging in front of his face in huge, white, billowing clouds.

Elora ignored him, humming a little tune and continued down the rows of books. Antoni frowned, confused as to why she would be leaving him when only moments ago she had said that she would jump into his arms at the first spooky thing that happened. This certainly counted as spooky and whatever the attraction staff were thinking in making this jump scare so cold, they were going to get several court cases against them without question.

"Elora!" he called out again, seeing that the girl had now disappeared around the corner of another snow-covered bookcase. Why was she suddenly leaving him like this? It made no sense to him, just like this whole scare attraction was now no longer making sense either.

Huffing in annoyance, as well as the cold, he scurried off after the girl, turning the corner to find himself facing a seemingly never-ending library of thousands upon thousands of books, all stacked neatly up in rows along the shelves. Antoni instinctually stepped closer and let out a gasp of air as blinding heat suddenly returned to him. He blinked and turned around, staring at the shelves he had just come from and now seeing the fake snow and ice with the air-conditioner hidden just out of view. A heavy gauze covered the initial area, making it next to impossible to see it before you walked face-first into what was essentially a fridge.

"Fuck sakes!" he cursed and turned sharply around, now annoyed at himself for falling for such a stupid, simple trick. "Elora! Why did you leave me behind? Where are you?"

There was no response, and Antoni was getting more frustrated by the moment. Antoni badly wanted to give the girl a good spanking and put her back in her place. She was being a devil, an evil trickster and she needed to be punished for her vile attitude and for messing around with him.

Stomping around a corner, the man let out a squeal like that of a high school girl as he found himself in front of a chair, in which sat the same cat-girl who had been following him around. Placing his hands on his hips, he glared at what he presumed to be a cast member who was merely sitting with a large, red, leather-bound book in her hands. She flicked through the pages with regularity that was a little too forced not to be practised. "Oh ha-ha, I get what you are now. Just part of this stupid story of this stupid place designed to spook us all. Well, guess what? It's not working anymore and-"

"Always so grumpy when you don't get your way," came the same monotone voice that had bothered him since the start of the attraction. "A character flaw that many would blame on anger issues or latent feelings you regret you had for your mother and sister…"

Antoni stormed forward to try and steal the book from the girl's hands, ready to grab her and give her a good shake to stop her talking. "Or more correctly, what you did not do to your perfect little sister. The one who was always a princess and always so perfect, but never allowed to be yours because incest is a sin that needs to be punished."

The book was pulled away from his outstretched fingers each time he tried to grab it before it was snapped shut. The cat-faced girl rose to her full height, which was barely five foot one, yet Antoni reflexively took a step backwards. "I know the blood that haunts your hands, the feelings you had when you enjoyed the screams and how even now, you can barely keep your hands to yourself."

"You're a fucked up little actor and once I'm out of here I'll…"

A charming laughter broke through the anger and Antoni whipped around to find Elora standing at the end of a bookshelf with a big, black book in her hands. "Why are you arguing with a trick mirror?"

Blinking, Antoni turned back to a reflection of himself but with a haunted, ghostly, ghoulish figure over the top. Clearly one of those interactive screens. He blinked and pointed. "There was that girl here again," he stated.

"Which girl?" Elora asked, sounding confused.

"The girl from the start, the one with the long, white hair, black and gold cat-mask who just keeps popping up everywhere!" Antoni nearly yelped.

Elora looked a little bit uncomfortable. "I think you're letting this place get to you, there's no one like that here."

"She was just..." He turned back and looked at the mirror once again, still showing the same strange goblin and let out a huff. "What is going on with me tonight? I hate these things."

"Aww, do they scare you?" Elora asked, sweetly.

"Never before, but this place is giving me the creeps."

A soft chuckle. "Says one who knows."

Antoni turned his attention back to Elora who was just smiling softly and indicated the book in her hand. "There's no key, but there is a riddle in here. If we can find the others, we should be able to solve it."

Antoni snorted, finding himself wanting to be with others just to prove he was not mad. Someone else had to have seen the ghost girl. Plus, his opinion of Elora was worsening every second. He wanted her, no doubt about that, but she was proving to be very much not worth his time.

She would not be moulded, she was already corrupted and that was not something he could stand.

"Yeah, let's try that," he said, trying to sound at least a little bit positive but not finding the will to really commit to it.

As he took several echoing steps towards the girl, that strange feeling from before crept over him. Elora's eyes changed to that sinister yellow for just a moment, her black lips moving to form the word "sunyata" and then there came a terrible creaking sound. Antoni snapped his head to the left and right, watching with growing terror as the spines of hundreds of books surrounding him creaked open with malevolent eyes in sour greens, fiery reds, deepest blacks, blinding whites, blood oranges and sickening purples with blazing pupils that stared directly at him.

Within seconds, the books launched themselves from their shelves, shrieking with unholy sounds and swooping into him or else biting at his hands, ankles, and feet. Antoni yelled and tried to bat them off. "What the fuck!"

"You're so pretty."

"A perfect princess."

"You don't need to worry about anything, I'll take care of it."

"You just sit there and don't say a word."
"Wear the pink dress, it's more flattering."
"You should not be out when you're bleeding, it's disgusting and makes horrible men want you."

"What do you mean, you don't like it? I prepared it just for you."

"You can't ever leave me."

"That's a bad girl, I'm going to have to punish you now."

"Oh shush, it's only a little pain, princesses like you can take the pain."

"If you don't stop squealing, I'll take you to the club where they'll strip you down and fuck you in all your..."

The books' chatter continued endlessly, echoing back words that he had said in the past. Antoni had no idea how this was happening. There was no way any of the attraction staff could have known! He was battered and bruised and there seemed to be no end in sight. He wanted to scream, to grab hold of something heavy and bash the books away but it seemed impossible to even move.

Until a beautiful, delicate hand reached out towards his through the chaos and he took it. The next second he was running, chasing behind Elora who seemed to know exactly where to go to escape from the flying books with their terrible words. They passed through several different aisles, scattering and dodging yet more books that came with their horrid words until the pair managed to exit the library through a doorway which slammed shut behind them.

Both Elora and Antoni were panting heavily, in a long corridor with large, painted canvases going all the way down. Both were silent for a few long seconds, taking deep breaths before they rose up at the same time. Within a second, Elora found herself backed up against the wall, with Antoni pressing so close to her body, his lips firmly on hers in a kiss that was filled with emotion as the terror drained away.

Antoni pulled back first, his eyes flashing with a well practised guilt. Damn his stupid thoughts from before, this girl was his perfect princess. A little on the wild side, different from all those other simpering little bitches but the one who would always be by his side. If he played his cards right. "I'm sorry, I don't know what came over me..."

"No, it's okay," Elora replied. "I've been wanting you to do that to me all night, if I'm honest."

Antoni's heart lurched in his throat. "Really?"

"Yes," Elora replied. "I snuck away from my father just for you."

Antoni gulped. "Won't he object to you dating an older man?"

"He'll probably burn you alive for even touching me, but I can handle him." Elora's reply held a note of confidence. "After all, I'm his perfect, little devil-angel."

About to put on the real charm, Antoni felt a presence behind him and turned sharply towards the paintings on the opposite wall. It was that damn tree with the swing on it, but this time the girl who had been haunting him was sitting in her spot. Although instead of a book being in her hands, there was now a dagger. The swirling grey slits of the cat-mask bore directly into Antoni's soul. "You should not follow the light, it will only bring your downfall, Antoni. Not that you weren't already doomed."

"Fuck off you bitch!" Antoni yelled, grabbing hold of Elora's hand, and heading down the corridor whilst taking several deep breaths to steady his nerves.

"She's creepy," Elora said with a shudder. "Who is she?"

"I've no clue, but she's been following me this whole time," Antoni replied, shaking his head. "Whatever this place's story is, it's really getting on my nerves now."

For a few long moments the pair were quiet as they made their way down the corridor until Elora piped up again. "But who was she, Antoni?"

Sighing through his teeth, the man tried to quiet the storm in his mind. It was natural that she would be curious, especially seeing as the strange figure seemed to know him more intimately than he knew himself. He didn't like where his thoughts were leading him either. There had been strange tales of late, about a collector who seemed to be stalking the streets. Regrettably he had not paid any attention to them because who believed in ghosts these days anyway? "I don't know. Presumably some overpaid scare actor who's far too into their job?"

Suddenly Antoni noticed they had arrived at two sets of stairs. One going up, the other going down.

"How the fuck is this place so big?" he asked out loud, looking for any indication about where he should go. He wondered for a moment how the others hadn't managed to make it here yet. If it was just as simple as stepping through a library door then surely his idiotic co-workers would have found their way by now. Elora's father would have probably been with them, which Antoni imagined would have caused issues, but that would have been a problem for future him to deal with. He had the girl firmly in his grasp now and no blustering man was going to take her away.

Elora chuckled. "They did say there are many paths to walk down at the start."

"But this is excessive!" Antoni's complaining made him sound like a spoiled little child who was not getting his way. "It's like a never ending hell."

"Isn't that what it's supposed to be? Never ending?"

"What?"

"Hell." A strangeness took Elora's voice as if it were speaking from the very depths of her stomach, but Antoni did not pay it the least bit of attention as he was looking at the two options in front of him.

Logically if this was a horror attraction then they would need to go down into the spooky basement where the freaks could come out to terrorise them for a bit and then find a way out. However, this place also seemed to have a merry time with changing the rules whenever the fuck it wanted so going up may be an option. Because who did not love creaking old attics with hidden boxes and the like? He sighed, tightened his grip on Elora's hand and started pulling her up the stairs. He figured at least they would get a bit of fresh air once they were at the top.

The door to the attic room opened instantly and silently, a soft breeze coming through which was refreshing but did not give any hints at what would be on the opposite side. Antoni braced himself, making sure to pull Elora a little closer to his side to be the big protector. Together they headed in.

Only to be mildly disappointed as there was just a pile of old boxes with dust and cobwebs on them. He peered into one only to discover it was empty. He frowned. "Did they not finish this place?"

Elora stared at him with terror and confusion written all over her face. "You don't see them?"

"What? The big, scary boxes?" Antoni sneered, letting go of the girl for a second as he checked another box.

"Antoni, please tell me you're joking?" Elora spoke, her words betraying the fact she was freaked out. "Or saying that there's nothing here just so I don't panic."

Rolling his eyes, he looked towards Elora. She was pale, shivering and clearly frightened out of her little mind but he felt nothing for her in that moment. Maybe a little bit of concern but he was so done with this place that he could not be bothered to play their silly games anymore. He wrongfully presumed that there was some pressure pad that Elora was standing on, making her hear strange voices or else triggering some hologram that he wasn't at the right angle to see. He sighed. "Elora, you're letting this place get to you again. It's all fake and illusory. These are just empty boxes that have nothing in them."

He would mention the pressure pad, but she would come around in a moment to see that she was just being silly. It did seem odd that her mood had changed so suddenly, though. It was almost as if he were suddenly dealing with a completely different person. It felt odd, but it could be that she was on her period because mood swings were a thing with that right? Not that he really knew, of course, because he didn't like being around females who were bleeding. It was not a great time to be around them, and they should really learn to be able to control it better these days.

"Antoni!" Elora half-screeched at him, completely terrified and out of her mind. "Please, just let me go…"

Blinking, Antoni turned to the girl who had been so wildly attracted to him less than two minutes ago and frowned at her. "Elora, stop being such a silly-minded thing. I'll show you that these boxes are empty."

He ignored her whining as he moved to the nearest large box, opened the top without looking in and then knocked it over.

A corpse landed on the floor with a wet squelch. The skin was a ghastly, pale colour and some parts of it were bloated. The thing's hair was long and ragged, soaked through. Huge black bruises stood out clearly in the shape of a handprint on the figure's neck and arms, the nails chipped and broken as if there had been a struggle. Antoni stared at it in confusion before a wheeze saw the creature heave water from its lungs and then begin the slow, difficult process of standing upright.

Each movement was punctuated with the creak, crunch, snap, or squelch of something that had not moved in a very long time.

It finally stood upright, the remains of a purple dress just cling-ing to the grotesque frame.

Antoni felt as though all the breath in his body had been sucked out of him as he stared at the horrible thing in front of him. Know-ing exactly who it had been.

Another box rattled off to the side, before tumbling down and disgorging another figure, this one clothed in a simple school uni-form but covered from head to foot in bruises that were in stark contrast to her pale skin. She rose up stiffly, almost as if it were a struggle to do so. Once she was upright, she had obvious trouble balancing due to one of her feet being twisted and facing back-wards.

A third crawled out from the darkest corner, her birch skin blackened further with soot that clung to her in horrible, long streaks. Her mouth opened to reveal broken teeth along with the markings of the rope that had been used to wedge it open all the way along the cheeks.

More boxes rattled and more figures appeared. They were di-shevelled, bruised, injured, half torn apart, and all were in varying states of decay. There were even two young men, though they had once looked extremely feminine, their arms caught together with barbed wire and their eyes gouged out. They made Antoni stumble back towards the nearest window.

"Antoni, what is this?" Elora screeched in a desperate attempt to have someone explain something. Antoni could not even begin to open his mouth. This wasn't real. No one knew about this except himself, and he hadn't done these terrible things to his precious, little princesses. It had been the other him who had done it.

He knew fine well that he had committed all these acts, and that once he grew bored of Elora that he would do the exact same thing to her. They weren't meant to belong in this world. They were too pure, too innocent and should be kept away from the likes of him. They were forbidden fruit, the ones that were so tempting and alluring no matter what other people said. He was drawn to their innocence like a moth to a flame. They shone so brightly, smiled so perfectly and were so precious that the very thought that they might one day leave him for some other man drove him insane. Even if they just happened to look towards a younger, more appropriately aged boy, Antoni would be filled with a harsh jealousy that would gnaw away at him for weeks on end.

This would lead him to start drinking, though not around his precious, little princesses, but when they were out of his reach. The envious green-eyed monster would start to boil at this point, the alcohol fuelling all the thoughts that made Antoni enraged. He would keep it locked up, let it simmer until it was boiling up in him and he could take it no longer. Then he would explode. It would only take a single little thing, one little word, one little action and everything would just spill out onto his perfect, little princess without a single memory of anything that he did.

He would just wake up in bed, with fresh bed sheets and no bad things in his apartment and then would be shocked to hear in the news of the disappearance of another young girl. Never did Antoni link them back to himself. Never did he consider that when he told others that the girl he was dating had left to do something else that his lies were so full of holes. Nobody really believed that. But no one really questioned him because no one knew who he was dating. He always protected them, kept them in the dark, so that those horrible men wouldn't do anything nasty to them.

Or more correctly, so that their fathers didn't come chasing him down the street with a pickaxe. That was a thing that happened with the first girl he had dated. Her dad was not happy.

But here, in this strange, creaky room which appeared to be connected to countless corridors that lead off from this blasted scare attraction, there was no running. No hiding. No lies.

All the precious princesses that he had dated and then destroyed were standing right before his eyes.

Antoni didn't need to pinch himself, didn't need to do anything to know that he was fully awake because even his worst nightmares had never held anything like this.

"Are you ever going to answer me?" Elora asked, her voice now calm and even, from the opposite side of the room.

The man shifted towards the sound, confused as he once again expected to find his perfect princess Elora standing there. She would be looking confused and sweet with all her pretty smiles, offering a hand to bring him out of this nightmare and back into her lap where he could rest, safe and sound. Where she would whisper sweet words into his ear, pet his hair and tell him that it was all a very silly dream that he had been having and that nothing could ever hurt him again. Then he would rise up, give her the most passionate of kisses that would make her exorbitantly wet. Then he would tear off all her pretty, little clothes and fuck her into an oblivion of sexual ecstasy.

Only to have his daydreams utterly smashed to Hell as his head was snapped to the side by a slap.

A snarl left him as he turned back towards Elora, ready to give her absolute hell. He was met with the strange, deep yellow eyes that had taunted him before in the library. This time though, they were clearly fixed on him, never wavering, and filled with such gleeful determination that Antoni felt the need to start running. Especially when a red-skinned hand grabbed onto his chin to forcibly turn his head to look at the figure a little fuller on. The long, black tail swished back and forth, like a cat who had finally caught up to its prey. "Now, sugar, I'll ask you once again. Which one of them would you like to drag you down to Hell the most?"

Antoni pulled back with a cry, staring at the mutilated bodies which were staggering towards him and shook his head. "None of this was me."

The devil-creature laughed. "Of course not, else why would *she* be hunting you down?"

A frown took Antoni, but just then a doorway at the other end of the attic flung itself open and he was not going to lose his chance. Letting out a herculean yell, Antoni charged straight towards the door, pushing past the mangled corpses and feeling nothing for them as they tumbled to the floor with muted groans of pain. Reaching the threshold he grabbed the door, slammed it shut behind him and then began to barricade the door with as many of the props as he could find.

"Oh, sweetie." The devil's voice came from the side, where she now sat on the ledge of a huge window. "Did you really think that was going to stop little, old me?"

Antoni picked up the nearest heavy object and threw it towards the devil. "What have you done with Elora?"

The she-devil merely moved to the side to avoid the thrown object, though she did tilt her head to the side in confusion at the question. "Is that really all you care about?" A snort came as more items were dodged. "Your miserable little existence is going to be over shortly and all you can think about is getting your dick wet?"

"You tricked me!" Antoni yelled, pointing at the devil with a manic stare in his eyes. "You pretended to be something that you never were."

"Just like you," the devil replied, getting down from the ledge and deftly avoiding all the items that Antoni was throwing at her. "Always playing the victim, always needing to be the one on top, always the one that was wronged or needed to be in the right. The liar. The cheat. The foul piece of human excrement that could never live up to Daddy's expectations, so you took it out on innocent lives who did not know any better."

Antoni found himself pinned up against the wall of the corridor, the devil woman directly in his face with her hands either side of his head. "The shit faced little fuck up who was nothing but a bane on everyone. Who never did anything of worth with his life yet expected everyone to just hand him everything on a silver platter. You're nothing more than a maggot who was trying to suck the life out of those who worked so hard and got things the honest way."

The rage came back into Antoni, because how dare this feeble creature make such accusations? Granted they were very true, and it was one of his deepest, darkest fears that he kept hidden from the world. He knew that he was never good enough, knew that he fucked up more than he ever solved in the grand scheme of things and that all his father's words about him were completely and totally true. But he couldn't let that be known, couldn't show the world his vulnerability because that would make him just like the rest of these useless fucks. He was not a sheep. He did not follow the herd. He lived his own life, and the world needed to pay him back for everything. How this creature could even have the audacity to stand there in front of him, saying those terrible things about him that did not match the image Antoni projected, the most amazing alpha male to grace the planet.

Antoni would teach her a lesson that she would never forget.

With a roar he grabbed onto her neck with both of his hands in the strongest stranglehold that he had ever done on anyone in his life. He felt the muscles of her neck contract, the windpipe bulging against his thumbs and heard the satisfying crack of the bones breaking. "Take this bitch, no weakling could ever take me down with words."

For a few seconds the yellow eyes just stared at him, the image morphing into Elora who looked so terrified and sweet that Antoni dropped her in shock. He stared at the beautiful girl, rubbing his eyes, and staring around the attraction. Everything was back to normal, there was no blood on anything, the door to the attic was closed but nothing was around to hold it in place and the window ledge was empty and still.

Slowly he knelt next to Elora, reaching out to brush her soft, glossy hair back from her face as he stared at her with no real feelings. "Oh, you silly little girl, what did you do to yourself?"

Antoni saw the dark bruises developing on her neck, the protruding bone which showed that her neck had been broken and he just felt empty. It was a shame that he hadn't gotten to taste her but that was a worry for another day. He decided that it would be best to head out, tell the organisers that there had been an accident and let them deal with the body because it wasn't his doing at the end of the day. It had been a very strange night, and he really did not want to deal with it anymore.

Antoni started down the stairs, only to pause when a flash of red and black landed right in front of him, yellow eyes ablaze whilst sharp teeth accompanied a manic grin. A forked tongue slipped out from between the lips to run up the entirety of his face. "Ohhh, do that again but harder, *Daddy*," the devil said, striking her sharp claws straight into his stomach. She immediately twisted them, dragging them along the length of his gullet before pulling back with a kamikaze scream that echoed loudly back at them.

Somehow Antoni found himself running, though it was more like staggering, through the dimly lit hallways, acutely aware of the raging demon behind him. She cackled and called after him, screaming about how she loved the chase, and he would never manage to escape her no matter what he did. Antoni ran on clutching at his stomach and praying for an exit.

One appeared in front of him, a door with a familiar green sign on it and he staggered through with a cry for help on his lips.

It died not a moment later when he found himself in a world of black and white, a single large, gnarled tree in front of him with a swing sitting unoccupied just swaying slightly in the breeze. Antoni let out a yell of confusion, turning back to grasp harshly for the door. But it wasn't there anymore. It had never existed in the first place, and he turned back towards the tree with a snarl.

"What the fuck do you want with me, you fucked up little bitch!" he yelled loudly.

Only to receive silence in return.

He stumbled towards the swing, barely noticing the blood that was pouring out of him. The colour was blacker than the rest of the shadows in this strange world and as he watched, it started to bleed together to form a dark path. Wearily he sat down on the swing, his eyes transfixed on the bloody path that was his creation as it expanded beyond the pure white cobblestones and formed a deep, shadowed doorway.

"Hi, sugar." The red-skinned demon who had been tormenting him the whole night emerged. She gave him an irritating little wave with her fingers, a wide smile on her wicked lips.

However, Antoni found he could not focus on her as the other one appeared. The white-haired girl who had followed him around, the one who had warned him countlessly not to follow the light. The girl with the black cat-mask that seemed almost too ethereal to be real. Antoni wanted to feel relief at seeing her standing there, wanted to scream at her to kill the red-skinned bitch and then come help him but a new feeling gathered in his gut.

Over the multi-layered, white dress, she now wore a hooded, black cape which was lined with symbols that he faintly recognised in gold and silver. The cat-mask remained the same, but the eyes now blazed a crimson red that shone with the beauty of a freshly cut ruby but dripped with the cruelty of a blood-soaked killer. In her hands she held a dagger, ornate looking with a faded gold handle. The blade was curved and held cut outs that would undoubtedly slip into the skin and then tear out in the most gruesome manner.

Antoni had never faced death personally, and whilst part of him was pretty sure that this was not literally the personification of death, it was clear that she was there to end his life.

He opened his mouth to speak but was cut off.

"Antoni Haswell," the monotone voice spoke, deep and ageless in the most terrifying of ways. "You are marked for collection."

Surprising himself, Antoni was able to stand up and hold his hand out briefly in a stop motion but before he could utter a single syllable, the girl from the painting was right in front of his face. It took him a second too long to realise that the sudden cold feeling in his throat was not caused by her strange aura. Once he realised what it was, the pain he felt as the blade was harshly yanked out was all-encompassing.

Antoni slammed to the floor, gagging for breath in a disgusting fashion as his body spasmed with the shock of it all.

The Collector stood and watched him for a few seconds, before turning away.

"Hey, aren't you going to bring him down?" the demon called, a hand on her hip.

The Collector paused. "Are you not contracted to do the very same thing?"

"Yeah, but you outrank me. I mean by a *lot*." The devil moved towards the thing on the floor, which was still squealing. "Don't want to be treading on your toes if I know what's good for me."

A slow blink came from the underside of the mask. "Who commissioned you?"

The devil paused, tucking a stray length of hair back behind her long, pointed ear. "His first..."

"Ah, you take him then," the Collector replied, turning back to face the door to leave. "That one needs more closure than mine... and I have what I came for."

The devil looked down on the squirming mass of a man who was still trying to get up and crawl away from his deserved punishment with no understanding of what he had even done in the first place. She gave him a firm kick, before smiling wickedly.

"Ya know, you are kind of cool," the she-devil addressed the Collector who was by now on the opposite side of the tree from her. "Some of the others said you were a pain to work with because you judge all, but I think we made a great team there."

A slight sound, which could have been a hum, it was impossible to tell, came from the Collector. "You were in the right place, at the right time, but I do not work with anyone."

"I know," the devil said. "If we meet again though, teammates?"

There was no verbal acknowledgement of either kind, but the devil did not worry about it. The Collector strode away, fading from view to return to whichever dimension she came from, leaving the devil alone with Antoni, who was still fighting for his life on the floor.

"Well, looks like it's just me and you now, huh, little Antoni?" the devil said, hunkering down next to the squirming mass of a man and smiling that wicked smile. "I've got so many people who want to have all the words with you when we get down there. It's going to be so much fun. Now stop being a whiny little bitch and come on."

Antoni had made it just to the edge of the black road and he let out a triumphant sound as he grabbed the edge, attempting to pull himself clear. The devil just smirked, grabbed one of his feet before rising. She immediately started walking, effortlessly dragging him away from the edge and straight to the shadowy door with a bubble of laughter escaping her. "Oh yes, we are going to have such fun. I can introduce you to all the ways that you let your victims die so you can experience them first hand and once we've gone through all of them, we'll just start the cycle over and over and over again until the very end of time. Because that's all you ever did, wasn't it Antoni?"

Antoni let out a long, agonised scream as he desperately grasped on to any edge that he could find but there was none in this strange black and white world. Soon the shadow gate loomed, and then he was through it. Into the depths of Hell where he would never be seen or heard from again.

At the entrance to the attraction, his workmates arrived and waited for their boss to appear, along with his daughter who was accompanied by a young man. He had kept a protective eye over her in the attraction, ensuring no harm would come to her. No one questioned why Antoni did not show up and when later he was filed as a missing person, presumed dead, none of them cared in the slightest.

Because they were all glad to be rid of the creep.

CHAPTER

Two

WHO CRIED MONSTER

The door slammed shut with such finality that Evan felt his heart breaking into a million pieces. He honestly thought that such a feat was impossible as his heart had already been destroyed since the day that his parents told him that he was going to be a big brother. The childish delight on their faces had been sickening, causing terror to shoot straight down to the very core of the eleven-year-old boy's being because he already knew what these two vile examples of humans could do to a single child. The thought of what they could do to more, was enough to make him almost consider running straight out of the door and to the world beyond.

But there was no point in doing that.

No adult ever believed him, even when he showed them proof. They just dismissed him as being at that age where he was seeking attention for himself, or else was doing something that he shouldn't be with the choir girls. He hated this village, hated the rules, and he hated that his sick and twisted parents could get away with everything that they did to him. All because they were the best friends of the village leader who was so blind to their actions that he put all the blame on Evan for trying to disrupt the peace of their beautiful community.

Evan was five when he realised that grownups were not to be trusted, and he swore to never turn out like them.

Even if it meant he had to follow all their rules, take whatever thing they felt like doing to him that day and never running away. As his father always said, "The blessings of the elder gods always favour the devout and one day they will be bestowed on you, our sacrificial lamb who never was."

He was six when he learnt that he was going to be a big brother, and Owena had turned up two days later. She was beautiful, serene and so quiet, especially for a three-year-old and even though he had been determined to not get attached, Evan had fallen hard for the girl who was to be his little sister the first moment that the pair of them were left alone. Owena had long, strawberry blond hair that went all the way down to the floor, freckles on her cheeks and tear-filled, grey eyes that just spoke of isolation and loneliness. Scooping her up into his arms, as she really was too small for her age, Evan had held her close and whispered, "I'm your big brother and I'll make sure they never hurt you. Ever. I promise."

The pair were inseparable after that, Owena following Evan around like a little, lost lamb and always obeying his instructions. He took the beatings, the burns, the verbal and mental abuse from the two morons who dared to call themselves his parents and he did it all for Owena. She gave him hope, something to fight for, something to live for, a reason to put up with all their bullshit because if the opportunity ever presented itself, he could get her out. Set her free, make it so that she could speak to adults who would listen to her because everyone listened to Owena.

He had just turned a completely ignored eight years old, when another announcement of becoming a big brother came to him. This time to a small, fragile little boy by the name of Joshua who had belonged to another set of parents in the village but now no longer. Evan had not questioned it, taking the frail boy into his arms, and hauling him to the kitchen to try to feed him something as he looked to be on the verge of death. Owena distracted their parents for a while, acting the perfect daughter before they got bored, and she came to help with feeding the boy.

Joshua was barely eighteen months old and so malnourished that Evan remained up with him the entire night just to keep feeding him the smallest amounts of milk. His parents kept on trying to force chunks of apple and carrots down the baby's throat, until Evan hid himself away in the basement where the monsters lived knowing that his parents would never dare to come down here.

They always told him horrifying stories of what the Beast would do to him if he were to become trapped there, but Evan knew better.

He did not believe in fairy stories of monsters and beasts. As far as he was concerned, there was nothing worse in the shadows than his parents and nothing could hurt him more than they could.

Joshua had survived that night and the one after that and continued to survive with the help of his big brother Evan. But he was slow to learn things, it took time and patience to really understand how he ticked which should have been frustrating, but Evan just couldn't be mad at him. Every time Joshua managed to do something on his own, learn a new skill, even just say a word was enough to fill the eldest brother's heart with more love and hope, even if he was bruised, battered and scared from what his parents constantly did to him.

He refused to allow the two adults anywhere near his siblings, fighting them at any opportunity that presented itself. He hid them both away so they would not see what was done to him and was always trying his hardest to just be there for them.

Evan got them food, clothes, some quiet toys for them to play with. He watched enviously as he saw others reading their little siblings' books or telling them about the magical place called school. Evan wasn't permitted to go there, for reasons that he could not understand as all the other kids in the village went to the school except them. Only once had he questioned it, before receiving the beating of his life that left him nearly dead in the corner of the room.

Owena had been the one to nurse him back to health, taking care of his wounds with precision and care whilst Joshua used his small size to get them raw ingredients, pots, and pans and eventually a small, little burner which allowed him to cook basic soups, omelettes and rice dishes on. How the pair had learned these behaviours, Evan did not know but he was so thankful for them.

It had taken many weeks for the eldest to be back on his feet again, and his parents still barely seemed to acknowledge his existence. The woman who had the audacity to call herself his mother had given him a strange look when she had found him in the bathroom, as if she did not even recognise what he was before shrugging and stating aloud, "Looks like the rotten meat is still clinging on."

The toothbrush that had been clasped in Evan's hand had clattered down to the sink loudly, but the woman was gone before he could even open his mouth to ask. A new type of terror surged through the young boy, something that felt completely foreign but also so familiar that he did not know where it had come from. But he knew what it meant, and suddenly everything clicked into place. He was not a child to his parents; he was not anything to them anymore because he had not been chosen. He wasn't meant to be here; he wasn't meant to have lived but the pair of them were too cowardly to get rid of him.

They had wanted him to be the centrepiece of the feast, and he hadn't been chosen.

Abandoning all attempts to continue cleaning himself, Evan had rushed almost blindly through the house and checked the yearly calendar that hung on the wall in the dining room. There were all sorts of marks on it, all key dates for what the leader said were the important events that would take place. Most of them sounded made up, or just adapted to fit in with the man's twisted sense of reality but there were two that were marked with such an extravagant style around them that they were impossible to ignore.

The Moon and Sun's Sacrificial Lamb Choosing was happening in three days.

Evan had felt sick, almost wanting to vomit right there and then. The choosing occurred three months before the Feast of the Immortal God.

Where the leader and his council would eat the corpses of two children.

Turning, Evan ran towards the room that he had inhabited for the past weeks with Owena and Joshua, letting out a quiet wail when he found them both still in the room. They were both alive and well, despite his struggles of taking care of them alone. Gathering the pair up into his arms, he held them tightly and allowed the tears to silently fall from his eyes. He knew what his parents were planning, what had probably been promised to them once again in exchange for their children and it made him feel more protective than ever.

If the pair were chosen, they would be killed, cooked and eaten by the village leader in a heinous ritual that Evan had no real understanding of. If they weren't, they would be subjected to the terror that had plagued Evan since the day that he was not selected. There was no fucking way that he was going to allow that to happen. The young boy of barely eleven was going to ensure that his brother and sister got to live the lives that they deserved, away from the evil madness of these fucked up adults who had no sense in their heads. There had to be something better out there, a world further than the woods where surely there were sane people who would help him.

He pulled back from the hug, looking at his two siblings before wiping away the tears from his eyes, "Gather what you can, we leave tomorrow."

The pair nodded silently before going back to what they had been doing before he arrived. Evan reluctantly stood up and took a deep breath. He could feel his father's presence behind him, assuming the man had wordlessly approached while Evan had been interacting with his siblings. Sharply, Evan turned to stare at him. The man towered over Evan, with a grim expression, short, cropped, black hair, sneaky little eyes and so many pock-marks on his face from acne that had never quite healed correctly. The man in front of him could barely fit in the doorway, his body too big, too awkward, and just all shades of wrong. This man used to terrify him, made him cower and whimper but now as he stood there, looking at the brute, holding an all too familiar beating belt in his hand, Evan only felt anger and rage.

This man was nothing but a coward, a bully who couldn't survive in reality and he would be forever a stain on the world. So, he resorted to the one thing that gave him a sense of belonging in this twisted and fucked up place. Being the leader's bitch and clamouring for his attention like the little fanboy he was. Otherwise he would have to accept that he had completely fucked up in every aspect of his life.

Part of Evan wanted to charge past this mess of a man, to run straight to the kitchen, grab the largest knife from the block and drive it straight into the man's heart. Then rip it out and go after his mother with the intention of slitting her throat. He shook with the notion of everything that he could do to these two bastards for all the things that they had done to him and for what they were going to do to his two precious little siblings... all thoughts jolted to a stop.

No, he wasn't like them, he would never do such a thing.

Though Evan wished that there was someone else who could, something that lurked in the shadows that could do all the terrible things for him so that he did not have to live with the guilt. He stepped towards the evil man in front of him, knowing what his fate was going to be without saying a word and for a moment thought of the Beast apparently locked away in the basement. What would that creature do if it got out, would it kill both of his parents or would it attack the whole village?

Evan lost himself in darkness as he was beaten once again, before being dragged through the house and then thrown into the basement he had just been thinking about. The sound that broke him out of his stupor was that of the door locking behind him and he started.

"What? No!" Evan screamed, rushing back up the wooden steps to attempt to push at the door but he knew it was hopeless. He clattered noisily back down the stairs, looking for any route out and finding only an extremely grimy window and a deadbolted access hatch that was locked from the outside. It did not stop him from attempting to push at the metal doors for the better part of an hour. When that didn't work, he began hammering at the glass with everything that he had until exhaustion and frustration got the better of him and he resorted to launching a rock through the window.

Sunlight streamed in from the gap, illuminating the dark, empty space in a golden glow that almost mocked Evan as once his eyes adjusted to the sudden change, it was easy to see that there was no way he could fit through it. A scream of rage left his lips, as he slammed his fists down onto the concrete floor and was hit by thousands upon thousands of different emotions that tore him to pieces.

A heavy, ground-shaking growl cut him off and Evan slowly raised his head. He shivered as his eyes fell on the large, black paw with silver claws and a rusted, old manacle around the ankle that landed in the beam of light that he had created.

The Beast was huge, virtually reaching the top beams of the basement and it radiated so much raw power that all Evan could do was simply stare at it. Fur as black as midnight, laced with blood-red streaks that seemed to emphasise the muscles on every last part of its body. The head was almost as big as Evan, with jaws that looked like they could snap an oak tree in half without so much as trying and long, silver-white fangs that glistened in the light. The deepest red eyes stared at the child in front of him with a deep longing question that seemed to strip straight through to the soul. Only the raw and painful truth could be shown to this creature, only the plainest of intentions and no one would ever be able to hide.

Evan found himself staring in wonder at the Beast, as well as pure terror because even the sight of this monster made him feel that his end could not be far now. No wonder they kept it locked up in the basement, away from everyone because it was clear that no matter what this thing was a killing machine. Though a strange impulse entered his heart and without understanding why, he reached forward with a hand as if to pet the Beast's head.

The Beast observed him for a few moments, tilting his head almost like a quizzical dog before lowering down slowly to allow the boy to touch his snout. Evan gasped at the surprising feeling of softness that came from the fur. It was so fine that it was tempting to just crawl forward and curl up to go to sleep next to this beast. Which was probably a very silly notion in the grand scheme of things because this was a killer and anyone trying to tame it would probably end up as nothing more than a pile of offal.

However, the creature just flopped down to the ground and wriggled closer, letting out a series of happy sounding grunts as it ever so gently placed its snout more firmly into Evan's lap. A heavy thumping noise turned out to be a tail that was wagging gleefully and for a few long moments, Evan was just completely frozen in place. Until the creature knocked his head towards Evan's hand and lightly pawed at his leg as if it were demanding to be petted. Breaking out of his stupor, Evan did not entirely know what to do at first but then hesitantly reached out to start petting the Beast who continued to wag its tail and make happy little noises.

This did not seem real to Evan, not in the slightest, and he wondered if he had somehow banged his head when he was thrown down the stairs. Or maybe this was the form that Death had chosen to arrive to him, to not to make everything so scary, even though the Beast was indeed a huge, extremely terrifying monster that could probably rip the entire village apart without even taking issue with it. But there was still a whole lot of pain in his body, his heart was still breaking into a million different pieces and once again the tears began to fall down his face.

A few of the water droplets fell onto the Beast's muzzle and the strange, dark red eyes turned towards Evan in what appeared to be a question. Without being able to rationally explain why he did it, Evan took a deep breath, "My so-called parents are trying to get my two siblings selected as the centrepiece for a feast where they'll be killed, cooked and eaten by the village elders for reasons I just don't understand."

The harshness of the situation boiled through his heart. "They've made my life utter hell for the past six years all because I didn't get selected for this 'great honour', as they call it. Now they think they've got a chance at it again they're going to pull out all the stops but neither Owena nor Joshua deserve what's going to happen to them."

"And I've tried to do everything in my power to stop them, I really have but I'm only one small kid and they're just big brutes who only care about getting attention from someone who barely even acknowledges their existence and...it's just not fair!" Evan continued bawling as he finally had a chance to release all the emotional turmoil that was contained in his heart. "I never did anything wrong, I followed their stupid rules, I made sure that everything was as it was supposed to be. There was probably never a chance in Hell that I would have been selected in the first place, so I don't even know why they tried to keep me around afterwards. It would have been easier to throw me onto the streets. I was five, I wouldn't have survived, but no they had to keep me around for whatever twisted reason they wanted to keep me around and now I've failed to protect the two I swore to protect, and it'll be my fault and just…"

A large, pink tongue lapped up across his face, hot breath smelling strangely pleasant but that could merely be because it was somewhat better than the vile stenches that haunted the house day and night. The boy blinked his soft, grey eyes in surprise, before looking down towards the Beast who looked back at him with so much understanding in those strange, red eyes.

The type of understanding that could only come from someone who had gone through a similar hell. Someone who had known what it was like to bow down to people who did not seem to make any sense and fearing the loss of a loved one. Someone who knew of taking all the pain, all the blame and trying everything to make sure that those they protected were safe when in the end it did not matter. No matter what, in the fucked up world that they had found themselves in, the evil was going to hurt those loved ones regardless of what they attempted to do.

There was always a moment when a choice was made, either to strike out or to shrink back, and Evan knew that he had indeed shrunk back in that moment. He could have acted out on his impulse to stab his father and slit his mother's throat; he had fantasised about it many times but just did not want to end up like them. If he killed them, what could he possibly do next? They had no way out of the town, the woods were thick, and he had no map or compass, and the elders would undoubtedly know it was he who had committed such a crime.

He was stuck forever in a loop of purgatory, unable to do anything because all paths lead to the same dismal end that he had no control over.

The Beast nuzzled him once again, before pulling back and changing into the shape of a man. Curiously, his human face was covered with that of the Beast, a mask with fine calligraphy in a purple-silver colour whilst the black and red fur cascaded down his long, slender back. The dark red eyes remained, whilst his body was covered with a tattered red robe with a series of black chains that wove across the man's chest in a type of pattern that seemed to frame the key components of his vital organs. For what purpose, Evan could not understand but for the first time in what felt like forever he felt no fear or the immediate need to recoil from an adult. Even if he had previously been a huge monster.

"Are you here to take me to Hell?" Evan asked, his voice even and controlled.

A shake of the head was the reply, followed by a pause as if the creature-like man was thinking about how best to respond. "I'm here to take you away from it," the guttural voice was more than enough to send shivers down anyone's spine, but it felt somehow warm and safe despite the roughness of it. "As well as your siblings."

"They'll come for us," Evan stated, with sadness in his voice. "Even if we escape, they'll come for us."

"Not if they're dead," the Beast responded. "Something which I think you long for and I can grant to you."

Evan blinked, sitting back a little. "What?"

"Those evil things upstairs, I can kill them all for you." The Beast stated matter-of-factly, as if he were offering to bring Evan a cup of tea, rather than the execution of his hateful parents. "As well as the others."

"The others?" Evan asked softly, not entirely sure how he should be responding to this situation.

The Beast nodded. "There are many like you in this town, Evan, too many who have suffered and gone unnoticed or uncared for. You're not the only one who's been locked away, beaten, tortured, and forced to raise siblings that you fear you cannot protect. There have been many before you, all unable to reach out because they did not believe that there was a way out. I've heard your pleas so many times, know the way you cry and wish for a better life for your siblings yet seek no reward for yourself. Now I can offer you the wish that you have wanted since the first day you became a big brother."

The boy exhaled.

"What price do I pay?"

The Beast smiled. "You've paid your price, many times over already."

"You're lying."

A deep chuckle came from the Beast. "You're perceptive but there is no price to you for me to do this. The price will sit on my shoulders alone and come the judgement day, only she will be the one to choose whether I stay by her side or fall."

There was an immediate temptation to ask who this she was, but Evan dismissed it as he stared into the red eyes of the Beast. Of the monster that had been sealed away in the basement, whom he had been told would unleash destruction and death if ever he got out, starting with him. The reality was that the Beast was the very death that the village elders feared the most. There was no running away from a creature like the Beast, there was no chance that he would just stop and never come back. If Evan unleashed him now, the whole town would be purged, and it would be a bloody massacre on a legendary scale.

"All the children will be saved?" Evan asked.

The Beast nodded. "Including yourself and your siblings."

Evan paused for a moment, only to see if he could see any other way out of this situation and found only death no matter which route he took. Taking a deep breath, he looked directly into the eyes of the Beast and found the only fitting words that he could say were, "May the blessings of the elder gods be on your side as you tear through the sacrificial sheep who should have protected their lambs."

A long pause occurred between the pair, the little boy looking up into the red eyes of the Beast who maintained a steely-eyed look with him. Whether it was a test or just a contemplation, Evan did not know but he felt the moment when everything shifted ever so slightly. The smile that was directed towards the boy was more of a smirk but one that was willingly received in that moment in time.

The elder man stood up, melting away to become the famed monster that could hardly be contained within the confines of the basement. The Beast stood still for a moment, then shook his entire huge body with a sound that could rival any earthquake that had been recorded. Heavy creaks and groans came from the foundations, an age-old crack ripping up from the bottom of the stairs heading straight up into the house.

Almost immediately there was a heavy hammering on the door, the deep voice of his father yelling, "What you playing at you little shit? Trying to explode the place with your little experiments down there?"

The pair exchanged a glance before Evan wisely stepped further into the shadows whilst the Beast remained where he was standing. "Answer me, damn it! You little turd! You know you must reply to me whenever I demand an answer out of you! Brat! What are you doing in there?"

The Beast sent his huge tail into the wall, a heavy thump that could not have really been caused by a child unless they were able to pick up the heaviest of washing machines and throw it. But the screaming continued, "What the fuck are you doing in there? Answer me now, you little shit! Don't make me come down there to unleash the Beast on you! Do you want to be bitten by the worst monster of your dreams? Do you?! Answer me!"

Oh the irony Evan thought to himself.

More tail whacks and a large paw swiped at the actual washing machine, which surprised Evan as he had no clue there was one down here. He had only ever been allowed to clean clothes in a cold bucket out the back of the house. The machine clattered heavily onto its side, some parts of it breaking off in the process, and the power cord groaned and stretched under the strain as, for a moment, it held the weight of the whole machine. Evan blinked at the appliance, before slipping further into the shadows behind the Beast without having to be told.

Blustering into the basement, his face red with rage at the disobedience on display, was his father. He wobbled down the steps, looking like a parody of a character mascot. He had greasy hair, tiny eyes that were some off-grey colour and a mouth with so many permanent frown lines it was not so hard to imagine him being a feeble, insecure wimp that begged for attention from the elders. He would probably do whatever they said as it fuelled some sick power play dynamic that he had fallen into years ago and was in too deep to get out of. The man probably did not even notice that he was trapped in this strange world, only obsessed with proving himself to be the best by presenting children to be eaten.

Evan realised that his fear had been misdirected towards this man, whilst he was an abusive arsehole, he was a self-congratulating cock who wanted all the attention but had no means of getting it himself. Someone who wanted to be included, to feel like they belonged, who had accepted the absolute wrong crowd because they finally got some validation. For a moment he felt a little bit of pity in his mind, but then he remembered all the freezing nights, all the beatings, all the horrible language that was directed towards him despite Evan being only a child.

The man was scouring the basement for him, squinting through the shaft of light into the shadows. "Where are you, you little shit? Show yourself so I can give you a spanking on top of the one that I gave you earlier."

A deep silence was his answer, the type that sent cold shivers down the spine of most people.

"Come out here now!" the man demanded like a spoilt child, stamping his foot in frustration. "You know to obey, you can't do anything but! I'll have to put you to work at the store or in the factory to pay off the damages to my equipment!"

The deep silence remained. Evan realised that the shadows were too deep to see through, though he was aware that the Beast had slipped away. He remained still however, not wanting to give anything away.

A tin can rattled off a storage shelf, clattering noisily before it rolled out of the darkness to the foot of Evan's father. He scowled at it before kicking the can away in a huff. Well, an approximation of a kick anyway. The can barely moved a few feet, and he whined at the pain in his toe. "You come out here right now, you bastard! I'm going to beat you so hard that you won't be able to walk for a month! And still, you'll do all your chores and service the feast because even though you're not the main attraction, you can at least be useful, you little-."

Two blazing, red eyes appeared in the darkness in front of the man, with black pupils and paired with large, bone-white teeth.

A snort escaped the man who sneered at the image. "Like something so pathetic as that is going to scare me, you shitfaced little brat! I've seen scarier stuff before and you're only delaying your punishment! Get out here now!" His voice was high-pitched and squeaky, so irritated that it really revealed the spoilt, little child who had demanded everything out of everyone but had never given anything back. The sort of man who thought that the world was just there to serve him, to give him everything that he never had because he deserved it despite never having actually put a lick of effort into it. The vile type of a person that took everything that they could, until the point where there was nothing left to take and then cried about how they were the victim in all of this because everyone always left them behind.

Without the understanding that it was all caused by their own behaviour.

The Beast was already tired of dealing with this worthless piece of human trash and moved towards him with clearly defined steps. They were soft and gentle at first, appearing to be like that of a timid child who would come crawling out to face whatever punishment this man wanted to deliver to them. Then there was the sound of a click at the very same moment that the Beast stepped into the small pool of light that had been caused when Evan's father had turned on the only bulb in the room.

The Beast's paw was bigger than the man's gut, his body broader than any creature that this pathetic human had ever seen, whilst his head towered over the man's tiny form like an impending shadow of doom that was lurking just out of sight, waiting to consume him. There was scarcely enough room in the basement for this massive creature, but it still moved gracefully as if unimpeded by the bulky mess that it had created.

Evan's father watched with growing horror as one large paw stepped onto the back of the prone washing machine, causing it to cave in on itself, scattering the internal workings as if it had been nothing more than a piñata. All the colour drained from the man's face as he stared, mouth agape at the monster in front of him. He tried to take a step backwards but found himself trapped by the stairs. Before he could process the thought of turning to run up them, the Beast was straight into his personal space, both paws blocking either side of the man whilst its jaws were right in his face.

Finally, the man found his voice, letting out an incoherent yell that may have been a slew of words but was more than likely just a high pitched call for someone to come and save him. The Beast sneezed on him, sending a mixture of moist, stickiness over the fat form as well as flecks of snot that were blacker than the fur surrounding him.

The man squealed like a suckling pig at the motion, trying to wipe the offending material off his arms only to find, to his mounting horror, that he suddenly couldn't move. Try as he might, the strange black substance locked him in place and then even pulled his body parts unwillingly closer to himself. His legs contracted together, arms crossing over as the black goo forced them into his rolls of fat which bulged out of the sides in a sickening display. But then all of that was being pushed in as well, his organs and bones were protesting at every movement, but he couldn't stop any of it.

The goo kept on pressing in on him at all sides, relentlessly, pushing everything inward and refusing to relent to his cries and tears of pain. The Beast watched as the man struggled, fought, and attempted to get free, but there was no way of escaping from the bindings that were now around him.

He slowly got smaller, shrivelling up until he was at least eighty per cent smaller than he had been before. His body was contorted in ways that should have been impossible and his fat, little head poked out of the top, still shrivelling with a scream that was mostly muted now due to the way his body was being squeezed.

The pressure stopped, but no relief was granted as the man's little, beady eyes followed the Beast's movement, knowing now that he faced his death completely and totally alone. The Beast almost had a flare of amusement in his red eyes before very slowly opening his jaws.

A final shriek was cut short by the Beast's snapping teeth crunching through the top of the cocooned man's head to rip him cleanly in two before throwing the top half away to land with a sickening crunch on the opposite side of the room. Stepping back, a paw swiped at the remaining ball of fat and sent it bouncing into the remains of the washing machine where it splattered itself with a squelch. But the Beast paid not the least bit of attention as he started up the basement stairs and into the main house.

Evan rushed out of the shadows, following the creature whilst not even acknowledging the body of his dead father. Why would he when only moments before he had been threatened with a beating for supposedly destroying the now dead man's property.

Plus, he had to find his little sister and brother before the deranged woman upstairs could do anything to them.

The Beast was standing in the kitchen, sniffing deeply and Evan squeezed past him, feeling no ounce of fear. "It's Thursday, so she'll be getting ready for the town hall gathering in her fancy room on the top floor," he informed gently, using a stool to grab a set of keys. "She won't have noticed the commotion here, she'll be too obsessed with her routines to care."

The Beast turned his head towards him for a second or two, before setting off into the corridor, his size adjusting with ease. Evan was fascinated but knew that he had to go and grab his siblings so they could get out without ever seeing anything. He could take the images of watching the two supposed grownups being slaughtered, as he wanted to ensure that they were truly dead as his soul was already damned to hell, but his baby brother and sister were at least going to get a chance at heaven.

Watching to make sure that the boy had indeed gone to wherever his siblings were being kept, the Beast turned his attention to the stairs and started up them with silent paws. The house stank of a vile perfume that seemed to seep into every piece of furniture or wall-fitting. Someone had clearly tried to make the place look impressive with items that were not of any real value, but someone whose opinion was highly regarded probably liked it. That was usually enough.

The Beast gritted his teeth at that notion, forcing back memories that tried to surface. He had a job to do and nothing could distract him from it. Evan had called for help, and he was here to deal with that call. He may be a little earlier than his masters would have wanted, but when had he ever followed the rules?

Pulling out of this silly line of thought, the black and red creature reached the top floor of the house where the strongest smell of that vile perfume mixed almost chokingly with an excessive amount of bleach and disinfectant. If one were to light a match up here, the entire place would go up in smoke in less than a second and burn all the occupants in such a blaze that there wouldn't even be dust left.

Shaking his head to clear it, the Beast headed towards the single set of double doors that were set with gaudy gold and silver designs. The wood crumbled as he barged his way through it, just at the exact same moment that a horrendous sound of a double-barrelled shotgun going off echoed throughout the house.

For a second the Beast paused, caught slightly off guard at the woman standing opposite him. She was tall, willowy and had floor-length hair that glistened with shine in a deep redwood colour that could only be achieved artificially. Tight-fitting clothes pinched and nipped at her body in such a way that couldn't be anything but painful and her heels were almost too tall. The overall look was like someone had turned a badly drawn cartoon character into real life and it was almost too hideous to look at. The Beast had seen some strange looking beings on his travels, and had dealt with the most vile pieces of scum that had ever walked the earth but this woman literally took the biscuit.

Though the Beast doubted that she could even eat a biscuit without it causing the biggest drama ever about gaining too much weight.

Her eyes narrowed into slits, regarding the creature that was right in front of her with nothing but contempt. "So," she drawled in an heavy southern tone, accent thick and heavy with the tar of the cigarettes that she clearly smoked more than she ever claimed, "this is what they sent to get me, huh? A lowly mutt?"

The Beast thought that maybe he should be offended by that remark but hunkered down lower with a deep growl instead.

The woman snorted, flicking a strand of her perfect hair back with a long, spindly finger. "I've seen puppies with a worse bite than you. If the Devil couldn't be bothered to come collect me personally then he clearly underestimated my prowess."

She raised the gun directly up towards the Beast's face. "This here is for my late husband, cause I don't doubt that useless brats squealing led you right to him. He wasn't the best man in the world, a pathetic worm that couldn't do anything right no matter what I told him, but he had his uses." The safety flicked off, "Don't take this personally, doggy, but a woman needs to take revenge for her man, despite how useless he was."

The shotgun went off, the bullets casting straight through the Beast's head.

"All my life I've been waiting for something."

Bang.

"Waiting for something better than his fat hide to come into my life and take me away from this."

Bang.

"Something to give me a purpose, you know?" The woman lit a cigarette and blew out a large plume of smoke that infested her rancidly clean smelling upper apartments.

"The elders said that I could have the greatest of things if I gave them a child to feast upon."

Bang.

"Just part of my flesh and blood. It sounded so grave but the more I thought about it, the more I was like why not?"

Bang.

"Afterall, what haven't I given that hasn't ever been paid back?" she finished, taking another long drag of the cigarette that was held between her lips. Pulling the white stick out, she exhaled a long plume of smoke and looked down at the pile of fur that stood at the top of the stairs. "Pity, you may have been some form of challenge, but I learnt a long time ago who the Devil sends to deliver justice and you certainly don't fit the bill."

Stubbing the cigarette out on a well-worn, oxidised, silver plate, the woman threw the shotgun almost casually onto her bed before stepping over the body of the Beast. The click of her heels virtually echoed as she headed down the stairs with a firm purpose in mind. She knew every single door of this house, knew all the hallways and where best to strike. The little brat would have gone to grab the offerings, under the delusion that he could get them out. He was a silly, little boy, but brave and fearless unlike his pig-headed father. She scrunched her nose as the smell of copper reached her, an uneasy feeling settling into her stomach at the thought of having to get someone to clean that up but then dismissing it because it wasn't her job to do such a thing. Her dainty, little hands did not get dirty because that was the way of life.

She turned right on the stairs and took two steps into the corridor before standing with her hands firmly on her hips.

Evan ran out of a door not a few seconds later, a large rucksack on his back that had been hastily filled with some clothes and both Owena and Joshua at either side of him holding onto his hands. They didn't notice her for a second or two, until Owena let out a gasp and Evan turned around with mounting terror in his eyes.

"Well, this is a delightful surprise," their mother said, looking at all three as they backed up immediately against the wall with pure, unadulterated fear practically dripping from them. "The big brother is trying to save the two younger ones. I could never have guessed you'd ever get the guts to try."

Evan seemed to find a moment's confidence. "Fuck off you bitch!"

It took less than five seconds for her to be across the space and slapping Evan across the face, her long nails digging into his cheeks to cause several nicks. "Be careful of your words boy, they may come back to haunt you one day."

Evan just glared back. "Not this time! Let us go!"

"Not a chance," she replied in her thick accent, grabbing Evan by the ear to start pulling him up as high as she could manage. Which wasn't that high given the stick-like nature of her arms, but Evan still whimpered and squealed like Hell. "These two are my ticket to a far better life and your scrawny little hide is not going to take that from me. No matter what dumb, crappy little hell spawns you summon to your aid."

Crash.

A table lamp with a terracotta base landed on the floor after having struck the side of the woman's head, causing her to shriek and drop Evan. Owena grabbed hold of Evan's hand and ran as fast as her little legs would carry her, Joshua copying by throwing an old ornamental dancing figure at the woman he was forced to call mother before stumbling off after the elder two with a cry. Evan was just able to get his feet back under him as his little brother arrived and they ran towards the stairs.

"You fucking little monsters!" screeched the woman, picking up and throwing ornaments of her own towards them. "Those are expensive! How dare you use them like that!"

The trio made it to the stairs and fled down them, ducking the occasional heavy projectile until they reached the front door. Evan yanked hard on it, aware that the chances of it being unlocked were next to none before digging into his pockets for the keychain that he had taken while collecting his siblings. The heavy clacking stomps of their mother descending the stairs brought a new wave of panic and desperation as more items were hurled their way despite their best efforts to not get caught.

Evan yelled as his mother's hand landed on his shoulder, hauling him backwards and he stared up into her angry eyes. "I'll teach you for sending the Devil down to get me, boy!"

"The Devil doesn't even care for your lost soul," a deep voice spoke from behind her, as a large paw slashed across the woman's back, cutting it open with gashes that were so deep nothing could survive them.

For a second, she remained upright, her lips turned into a scowl that could only be described as filled with nothing but the bitter taste of shit before her brain finally caught up to what had just happened. The scream that she let out was from the very depths of her soul, but it lasted maybe two seconds before it cut off, as her lifeless body crumpled to the ground in a big useless heap.

Evan managed to get the key into the door to unlock it, not caring what happened to the woman as he hauled it open and tore out onto the streets. The sting of cold air was almost a relief to his system, but he could not stop now. They had to get out. He turned left and right, checking for any signs of life but only finding the church which was lit up like a celebration display with so many lights all twinkling and the sounds of merry making coming from inside. He narrowed his eyes in distaste towards it, not even caring for the reason why there were so many people celebrating and pulled his two siblings towards his chest. "We'll head for the bus on the far end of town, I don't know when it'll run but... hey, wait, where are you going?"

The Beast had carefully stepped over the children, towering over them all again with fresh blood on his massive paw. Evan didn't need to guess where that had come from as he had heard the crunch of his mother's body. He only hoped it had been her head that had been crushed underfoot with that delightful sound. It was sure to haunt his dreams, but that was something to worry about at a much later date. The Beast was heading straight towards the church, his entire being rippling with anger and intention to destroy.

Evan wanted to call out to stop him but decided against it. He had more pressing responsibilities right now. "Thank you," he whispered, tugging on Owena and Joshua's hands to get them going. However, Owena broke away for a few seconds, catching up to the Beast only to latch onto his leg in a hug. The creature turned to look at her, a soft expression on his face as he gave her a big, wet lick much like a dog would before gently nosing her away. The girl smiled and hurried back towards Evan who took hold of her hand again and started running in the opposite direction.

Turning back towards the church, the Beast narrowed his eyes and then stalked directly towards the building. Evan may have only summoned him to deal with his parents to save his siblings from a terrible fate, but there were too many innocent lives that had been played with here. The Beast did not like cults, especially ones that were run by scumbags who wanted to control the world. Some of the adults were innocent. Just fools who had been manipulated into this situation by a silver-tongued devil who would exploit their biggest fears to bring them straight into his lap. Most were grabbing bastards who saw opportunities. The Beast saw them all as monsters who needed to be eradicated, and no one was going to stop him following that path tonight.

He was less than ten paces away from the church when the screaming started. He hadn't even let out a warning growl because there was no need. Within moments the glass in most of the windows was shattered, as at least twenty guns pointed out towards him, and started unloading. The bullets pinged off the path, fences, broke through windows, and decimated some garden statues. Of course, the Beast remained unharmed and began to pace around the church examining it with a calculated gaze.

It would be easy to just charge in through the doors and tear every last one of these useless mother fuckers to pieces, but it would be time consuming, and the Beast did not feel it was required. It would also give the opportunity for some of the brighter ones to escape and there was no way that he was allowing that. He noted a cellar, with one exit that was quickly dealt with as he hurled one of the prominent statues straight onto the door with a single swipe of his paw.

The glass in the windows kept on smashing, more gunfire being directed towards him, but the Beast did not care or notice it. Mortal weapons could not physically wound him, though he liked to have fun and pretend that they did on occasion. The Beast was a little concerned with the number of bullets that they were using as they were going to raise a lot of questions. Though he did not dwell on it for too long.

On the farthest side of the church, he found exactly what he needed.

At least three hundred crates of alcohol, all neatly stacked up in rows all the way up to the side of the church. A howl escaped him, deep and melodious. Then, coming straight from the depths of Hell through his paws, there creeped out thick, black, winding thorn branches that slithered the whole way around the building. They grew quickly and densely, blocking out the light from any nearby source.

One brave soul appeared on the outside of the church, brandishing a crucifix and calling some ancient language that was meant to drive the Beast away.

He took two steps forward, regarded the scrawny, little man for a second and then cleanly snapped his head off. The screams from inside the church became louder now but the Beast ignored them, instead stepping back to ensure that the vines finished growing as they should. There came yells of despair as someone was clearly trying to use the cellar escape and not realising that it was all for nought.

Shots were still being fired at him, just how many bullets these people had was staggering, but the Beast merely stood in place and waited. Eventually the vines had completely engulfed the whole of the church, covering it in an inky darkness that crept out of nightmares.

The elder strode towards the doors. "Is that monster still there?"

"Yes," stated one of the men, squinting blindly ahead. "Leastways I think he is. Hasn't moved since he took the priest down."

The elder shuddered. "How is that possible? What can we do against it?"

"You're asking me?" the man asked, turning to stare in almost disbelief at the man he had followed for years and wondering if this reaction was fear or something else. "You're the one who-"

"Shut up! Just get rid of that thing! Keep firing!" the elder shouted, moving rapidly to bolster the others but with a wavering tone that was noticed by many. They started to lower their weapons, staring at the great man who had brought them there, so full of poise and grace, knowledge, and power, starting to shiver like a leaf. The man who had given them the teachings and had shown them the path to glory and salvation. The man who was now pale, intimidated, and scared. He wasn't giving them divine insights, wasn't telling them that their gods would come and smite the vile creature that was outside and destroying them. He was staggering around in a complete panic, like a headless chicken, seeming determined to get out and save his own skin.

The elder reached the main door, which had been barricaded up and started pulling things away, squealing like a suckling pig that was going to be slaughtered. He didn't want to die, he hadn't done anything wrong and he wanted his mother.

The gunshots had stopped a while ago, whilst his whole congregation just stared at this pathetic lump of a man as the penny finally dropped for all of them.

Some sat down in shock, others emptied their bullets out whilst several others took one look at the inky blackness outside and took their own lives before the real retribution came down on their eternal souls.

With a final crash, the elder finally got the barricade away from the doors and hauled them open with a cry of release from a hideous torment.

Only to find himself staring at a man in a tattered red robe, with black chains across his chest and a mask of the beast that had howled at them. The crimson eyes were alight with the flame that came from a lit rag at the end of a bottle of extremely expensive wine that had been brought in especially for the Lunar Feast.

"Not a word," the Beast said, before smashing the Molotov cocktail straight on top of the elder's head. His scream was the first of many that filled up the night sky, the smoke curling up into the stars in a thick, choking haze that bothered nobody. The flames engulfed the building bound by the vines, causing only flashes of red and orange whilst billowing out a heavy, black smog towards the night sky.

The Beast stared at the mess and then released an all mighty howl towards the darkened sky, though whether in celebration or anguish was anyone's guess.

Evan turned his head briefly towards the sound, but at this end of the town it was impossible to see anything but the bus stop that he was now waiting at, clutching onto his two siblings tightly. An odd sort of feeling passed over him, almost as if a great burden had been lifted from his shoulders but he wasn't entirely sure what it was.

The sudden sound of a bus pulling up made Evan jump and he turned, surprised to see a very new, large, and shiny coach arriving at the stop. The door opened and a man, with white cat-ears and a tail stepped out with a smile on his face. "Ah, perfect timing. Let's get you onboard, shall we?" Nexus said, his voice soft and calm.

Evan blinked and nodded, knowing instinctively that he could trust this stranger though not knowing fully as to how. Though once Owena and Joshua were on board, a thought occurred to him. "What about the other children?"

"Right here," came the deep voice of the Beast, the human version of whom Evan had briefly met. He was surrounded by the other children of the village, most were still in the process of waking up, or dropping back off to sleep.

Nexus smiled. "Welcome onboard then."

It took little to no time for the children to be loaded safely into the seats and Evan turned back towards the Beast who seemed to be watching something in the distance. On an impulse he rushed towards the creature, threw his arms around his middle and held on tight. Just like Owena had done much earlier. "Thank you."

"No need," the Beast said. "Just grow up to lead a good life, that'll do me."

Evan smiled and turned, heading back onto the coach to grab hold of his siblings once again and hold onto them tightly. He had no idea what the future would hold for them now, but he was sure that it would be far brighter than it had been before. The coach pulled away from the town.

"Did you kill all of them?" Nexus asked.

"Yes," came the straightforward reply.

"Then rest, friend," Nexus said softly, even though he knew what was coming.

The Beast did not answer him, merely changing back into his creature form and stalking off into the night. Nexus watched him go silently, before letting out a breath. "The sun and moon always follow one another, but never catch up."

He turned and went his own way, knowing that soon he would hear from one of his two charges. He knew that they would never give up on their personal paths of redemption.

MAZE OF PERFECTION

"It's a simple task," the monotone voice was saying as Malcolm Kennedy and his wife Celeste stared around the strange world that they found themselves in. It had been a very strange day, followed by a night that made little to no sense to either of them. They had both left early for work in the morning, as per usual, with their lunches prepared and breakfast dishes left on the side to be dealt with by the urchins. Malcolm had taken the car, as the drive would be soothing to his tired soul, whereas Celeste got picked up by her preferred chauffeur company as there were several stressful high-end meetings that had to be attended today that could see another increase of profit if they went smoothly.

They had both arrived at their workplace and set about their tasks.

But there were loads of little things that were wrong, out of place or not up to their high standards. The coffee had been switched to some cheap, instant brand, the flowers were not fresh as they had arrived yesterday and the cleaner had left a line of dust on the topmost bookshelf, right in the most difficult to reach corner.

Malcolm found that his computer password no longer worked and he was unable to access anything until late afternoon. Then it transpired that a virus had wiped most of his important files and had emailed a bunch of other documents to a place that could not be tracked. He had been furious, stomping around, demanding answers, and making threats to everyone's jobs as if they were the ones who had personally caused this mess. Only one person pointed out the fact that according to the employee tracking software that was installed on all the computers, which Malcolm had insisted on as he wanted to ensure that his employees were always constantly working throughout the day, there was ample proof that the boss had arrived at work yesterday, logged into his computer and then immediately left for a day-long lunch date. The irony in this was that Malcolm could often be heard declaring that, "Working without break is how I got to the position of being your boss." Despite this he was regularly 'out of office' with several lunch dates that were certainly not beneficial to the office environment.

For Celeste, her day was filled with constant delays, cancellations of meetings and a series of bad project reviews that were popping up everywhere online. There were articles, company reviews, problematic social media posts and witness statements that just seemed to appear out of nowhere and were trending on all the most popular and important websites. To make matters worse, she could not get onto any of her own social media accounts, as someone had evidently discovered her password and changed all her details. Even if she tried a password reset, it went to a completely different email address that she had no access to. She had stormed about in her green, tweed, pencil skirt, screaming down her phone for half the morning and demanding that her secretary sort everything out. She also spoke to the lawyers who were suddenly not as friendly as they used to be and seemed to be working against her. Someone was trying to spoil her day, and they were going to pay for all of this once she got her hands on them.

At three-thirty, the couple had met up to have an executive meeting in one of the most expensive restaurants in town and downed at least four bottles of fine champagne between them. Unfortunately, their credit cards were declined when they came to pay their tabs, so after a long and difficult phone call with their bank and the threats of police they eventually left with rude comments and a shouting match that was beyond vile. In fact, there wasn't even a word to begin to describe the words that the pair used as they climbed into a car, not theirs, and drove off into the night.

Eventually they had found themselves on a long, black road, in the middle of nowhere with a glimmering white wall in front of them. Both had stepped out at the same time, confused now that they had both relaxed a little. It wasn't every day that you came across a wall blocking the road, after all.

"Well, this just takes the uttermost piss on top of everything else today," Malcolm had drawled.

"It's a simple enough task." A cold, monotone voice came from a small figure behind them. The figure was wearing a midnight-blue dress, which was partially overlaid with a darker velvet material. The velvet was adorned with silver detailing and the skirt of the dress had a triangle cut from the front, revealing a black, multi-layered petticoat. She walked towards them as long wisps of

Nordic-white hair tumbled out of a midnight-blue cape, lined once again with silver but this time appearing to be a multitude of religious symbols and patterns all woven together. A cat-mask of two colours, one of white the other a black, was lined with gold in patches that looked rusted with some dark red material that neither Malcolm nor Celeste could identify. "Get through the maze, with your life intact, and you can return to the mortal realm."

"Return to what?" Celeste asked snippily.

"I would start running now," the monotone voice of the Collector continued, pulling an ornate, silver pocket watch out of a hidden pocket with an almost skeletal hand. "You've already lost thirty seconds."

"I do not know what kind of prank you think you're pulling, missy," Malcolm started, using his superior voice that just made him sound like he was compensating for a whole lot of things in his life. "But you had better start explaining why..."

"One minute gone, you're doing such a terrible job of following simple instructions," replied the Collector, the soulless grey eyes looking up. "Especially with the dogs coming for you both now."

About to start getting angry, Malcolm instead found himself stopping short when the sound of heavy breathing came from behind him. Turning his head, he did not have a moment to start screaming as two of the largest dogs he had ever seen, with teeth as sharp as razors howled before charging forward, their murderous intentions incredibly clear. He did not even make it two steps into a run before he was set upon by the first dog, its claws and teeth tearing into him in a matter of seconds. His life ended in a painful series of tears and scratches.

Celeste screamed and staggered on her high heels, towards the open doorway of the maze but crumpled down to the ground not a moment later as the second dog caught up with her and tore open her back. She screamed violently, feeling the blackness hit her almost instantly.

Silence.

A sharp intake of breath.

A high-pitched wailing sound

A freezing sensation.

Colour bled back harshly into both Malcolm and Celeste's eyes and minds, as both found themselves standing upright, back in the clothes that they had been wearing with no wounds or injuries. They were back at the gateway to the maze, the strange figure in the midnight-blue dress and mixed black and gold cat-mask watching them. "It's a simple task," she repeated with the same cold monotone as she had done before. "Get through the maze with your life intact and you can return to the mortal realm."

Malcolm turned to look behind him, seeing the dogs some distance off but pulling on thick, heavy leads that were holding them in place. Seeing sense, he turned back, grabbed Celeste, and pushed her forward into the maze. "It's just a maze, we can make it through."

"What the fuck is going on?" Celeste asked, unsteady in her heels as she tried to pull her arm out of her husband's hold. "Malcolm, you can't be serious about doing what this witch says?"

"Want to be eaten by dogs again?" Malcolm demanded, pulling Celeste along.

The woman fell silent for a moment or two, still clearly fuming about something but right now Malcolm could not deal with his wife's temper tantrum. Today had been already straining enough Celeste thought, and whatever prank this was, their children were going to pay for it once she and Macolm got out the other side. Because it could only be them that were doing this sort of useless task that took away from the day. The lazy little bastards that they were.

Malcolm was also hiding his own fear behind anger, because that was the way that he had survived so far in the world, and no one was ever going to call him a little scaredy cat ever again.

The walls of the maze were grey and imposing, almost impossible to navigate as everywhere looked the same. Finally, Celeste was able to pull her arm away from Malcolm and stomped forward. "Why are we even doing this?"

"Because it's a simple task," Malcolm mimicked the girl from before. "We have to do it."

"That's not an answer!" screamed Celeste, stamping her feet. "It's just repeating what-"

She was cut off rather abruptly, but not by Malcolm who had sorely wanted to. Instead, she was cut off mid-sentence by the swiftest, sharpest, and most silent of swinging saw blades that sliced the woman cleanly in half. The two halves of her body split and dropped to the floor exposing her guts and other vital organs as her innards splattered and fell apart.

Malcolm threw himself back in horror, looking at the mess and then yelling as another swinging blade passed by him, catching the edge of his jacket suit to miraculously only rip the fabric. He let out another yelp and pushed himself off the wall, running wildly down the long corridor, feeling the swinging blades rush past him multiple times in silence. Any one of them could have ended his life.

He made it down to the end and turned left, staggering back with sounds he would never admit to having made out loud as the panic boiled over. This couldn't be real; this couldn't be happening. Coming to a stop, he took several long, deep breaths to calm himself and then peered around the corner to see that the blades were still swinging, and the two halves of Celeste were laying where they had fallen. He whimpered like a wounded dog before turning around to walk away, only to find himself faced with a rusted, burnt-smelling metal grid wall. Experimentally, he reached out to touch it and regretted it when the heat scorched his fingers. He pulled back his hand with a yelp, realising that he could not go that way and turned to walk out.

His way was blocked by another matching grid wall which had not been there previously.

All the colour drained from his face as the second grid wall moved towards him with an unsettling quickness. Almost instantly he felt the hot metal burn into his skin, blistering and cooking it within seconds whilst he was squashed flatter than a pancake and felt every bubble before it popped with his blood all over the bars.

Silence.

A sharp intake of breath.

A high-pitched wailing sound

A freezing sensation.

"It's a simple enough task, you can easily complete it if you think about it," came the monotone voice of the strange figure in the blue dress. "Pass through the maze with your life intact and you can return to the mortal realm."

Malcolm and Celeste stared silently at one another, before turning to stare at the strange woman who was giving them instructions. She was looking at a gold pocket watch this time, more interested in that than either of them. "You've lost thirty seconds again," she chimed out.

The dogs began braying loudly and Celeste reacted first, kicking her shoes off, grabbing hold of Malcolm's hand and dragging him back into the maze. The first corridor was exactly as it had been, plain, grey walls and as they rounded the corner the woman stopped. Five seconds later the first blade swung silently through the air, and she turned to Malcolm. "What did you do after this?"

"Err," Malcolm stammered, fearing for his life as he watched the blades move back and forth.

Celeste snapped her fingers impatiently in front of his face. "Think man, you had to have gotten a little further than me."

"I didn't," he answered in a weak voice. "I ran blindly and then went left and ended up cooked." His face paled at the thought, but Celeste grabbed him again.

"Fine, we go right at the end and get through this sick and twisted little game," she stated outright. "We can do this with no hassle if we just keep it together. Don't you dare start throwing up on me."

Malcolm was still pale, but he nodded and stared ahead with vacant eyes. Celeste rolled her own and was the one to move them down the corridor of blades, pausing strategically to count and ensure that they did not get sliced in half again. They reached the end of the corridor, the putrid stench from the left more than enough to put them off so they set off to the right down the other corridor.

This one looked clear, but the pair had learned to not blindly trust that anything was as it seemed right now. Neither one of them could even begin to explain what the hell was going on but neither of them wanted to stick around for long enough to work it out either. Today was a strange one, that much was certain, and they needed to get through whatever this crazy ass shit was before deciding what to do about it. Malcolm was already formulating in his brain what he could possibly sue the perpetrators for, whereas Celeste was ranking the possible employees that needed firing and which child was going to get a spanking for this. It had to be one of the children who was messing around with them right now, there was no one else who would dare.

The corridor was quiet. Entirely too quiet. Neither of them trusted it.

"What's going to happen?" Malcolm whispered, frightened that if he broke the silence then something would come and get them.

"How should I know?" Celeste snapped back at him. "It's not like I have a map or anything actually telling me what we're facing in this godforsaken shithole."

Her foot suddenly went down, a small depression appearing in the middle of the path that she was in. An arrow shot across the brow of her head, the side just catching Malcolm's cheek and drawing blood almost instantly. He let out a banshee scream, flinging himself to the side with a wail as though half of his face had been ripped off.

Letting out a groan of frustration, Celeste moved towards him and slapped him across the face. "Stop with that wailing, let me have a look."

"I've just lost half my face!" Malcolm screamed like a baby who had just had the candy taken off him. "It hurts!"

"If you would shut up for a minute, I can check." Celeste tutted, grabbing his hand and pulled it away from the blood-soaked mess. In the meantime, she rammed her knee into his stomach and with her other hand grabbed his hair and yanked his head to the side so that she could get a better look at the injury. Sneering, the woman shoved her husband back against the wall, scoffing loudly as she said, "It's barely a scratch. Stop being such a baby about it. Clearly, we must watch out for setting off the traps, so you go in front."

"Why me?" Malcolm whined.

Celeste pouted. "I'm the poor defenceless woman, you're a sodding oaf of a useless man. Keep your head low and we'll get through this and then teach that creepy bitch a lesson afterwards." When Malcolm did not move, she grabbed him by the collar and hauled him in front of her, kicking his backside for good measure to get him going.

Malcolm was stuttering and panicking the whole way down the corridor, terrified of even coming across one more pressure plate. However, they made it whilst only setting off one more arrow that whizzed harmlessly over their heads as they both ducked down low.

The corridor split off into three at the bottom, all of them in the same cool, white granite that the rest of the walls had been.

Malcolm whimpered. "Where do we go?"

"You're in the lead, you choose," Celeste whined.

"I'm injured and not in full charge of my faculties," Malcolm argued back.

"You can see further," Celeste stubbornly replied.

Malcolm wanted to point out that he couldn't see very much beyond anything that was within his line of sight but knew better than to try and argue with his wife when she was in this mood. It was like trying to convince a small, yappy dog to give up a bone. They get snippy, bitchy and then bite your ankles for the next week to teach you a lesson.

On a whim, and with a big whine, he set off down the left-hand tunnel as last time it had been the correct choice.

For the first few hundred steps, it all seemed to be just the same white granite walls with nothing too remarkable until the corridor looped around to the left and the pair found themselves faced with a very solid wall. Malcolm frowned and raised his head as he looked up to try and see how they could climb it. Clearly that was not an option because two seconds later, a huge slam came from behind them and another very solid wall had closed them into the end of this area.

"What the fuck?" Celeste yelled but stopped at a rotating, clanking sound. It was like a chain pulling open something very heavy. There was a rushing cascade of water that sizzled and stung in the most unpleasant of ways.

She turned around, spluttering and stuttering towards Malcolm, only to let out her own horrific scream as she saw the half-melted form of her husband being swallowed up by the same acidic water that was slowly eating her alive.

Silence.

A sharp intake of breath.

A high-pitched wailing sound

A freezing sensation.

Celeste blinked repeatedly and turned to stare at the strange woman who was still standing in the same spot. Her lips formed the usual statement. A feeling of dreadful familiarity crossed over Celeste, but she did not waste time, instead grabbing hold of Malcolm who was screaming incoherently at the other woman and started running the maze again.

Malcolm kept on whining like a boy who had been forced to share his toys, but Celeste ignored him completely. She focused on avoiding the dogs, the swinging blades, taking the right turn so as not to come across the burning wall, heading down the corridor with the push pads that activated arrows, activating two in her haste to get through them and reach where they had been before. She continued to ignore her husband's whining. They had to focus and she chose the right hand passage because it just felt right.

"Will you do me a favour and shut the fuck up?" Celeste finally shouted as she let go of her husband. "Honestly, all you do is complain all of the time."

"Well, I have a right to complain," Malcolm stated in his most bratty voice. "We're being forced into this maze where we're constantly dying and if we don't get caught by traps, we get eaten by dogs and there's no reason for it. I am the CEO of a big company and I already have enough stress to deal with. This little game isn't helping with that, and I know for a fact that everything today has got to be a scheme from those little bastards at home. We haven't been giving them enough to keep them occupied. They're getting big ideas and-"

Celeste turned and slapped him hard across the face. For a moment afterwards she hesitated, remembering that where she had slapped him had been an open wound not so long ago. She sharply shook the thought away.

"Get your head out of your arse, Malcolm," she snapped at him. "We don't stand there whining like fucking children, we are proactive and learned to deal with the problems that come our way through hardship and pain. We set the rules, give the direction that they need and if they get things wrong then it is their own fault."

She took a deep breath. "We are not in the wrong here. We are the victims of a cruel prank and once we're out of this mess, we shall go back and make them deal with the consequences of it. Right now, we have a task to get through this maze alive and then we can go home. We can do this if we focus and keep a level head.

We are superior, and they have no idea how to handle the intelligence that we possess."

Seeing that her husband was calming down and focusing, she smiled condescendingly towards him and patted him on the head. "Now, we are going to not lose our heads and we're going to get through this without any more whining, or arguments, or issues. We're better than this stupid, little maze, aren't we?"

"Yes, dear," Malcolm stated, sounding more like the powerful man that she knew he could be.

"Good," Celeste said. "Though when we do get out of here, our children will know about it."

A nod was her response, and the pair set off again, determined that they were going to do everything perfectly right from now on and nothing could stop them.

Until they reached another apparent dead end but this time there was a wall with what appeared to be some kind of block puzzle. There were different coloured dots, squares and triangles that were all mixed up on the individual tiles. Next to it was a plaque that read, "Reverse your meaning as this test is only for those who truly know what they have done. Connect the dots to escape, the squares to see sense and the triangles to admit defeat."

Malcolm cracked his fingers. "Ah, good, old twister puzzles. I was the best at solving these in school. Even won an award for them back in the day."

"Well good, you can solve it then and we can escape," Celeste placated.

So, with an almost childish glee, Malcolm started twisting the various panels to start matching up the dots with a series of clicks. Only when the last one was done, the wall fell backwards on itself and unleashed a hellhound on the pair of them who promptly ripped them apart limb by limb.

Silence.

A sharp intake of breath.

A high-pitched wailing sound

A freezing sensation.

The second time they returned, Malcolm connected the squares in a hurried fashion, panic clearly rushing through his brain. This time the wall dissolved and thousands upon thousands of termites crawled out, sweeping up around their bodies and slowly ate them alive until they were nothing but dust.

Silence.

A sharp intake of breath.

A high-pitched wailing sound

A freezing sensation.

With the triangles came a momentary silence, before multiple hands reached out of the rocks to grab hold of both Malcolm and Celeste and drag them both down to a burning pit. The wails and moans of thousands of those who had come before were horrific to hear and drowned out both of their screams.

Silence.

A sharp intake of breath.

A high-pitched wailing sound

A freezing sensation.

Malcolm staggered into the three-way corridor, yanked Celeste closer and headed up the remaining passageway in the faint hope that this nightmare would be over soon.

He could still hear the chilling laughter that had come from the girl at the entrance. "So simple a task, that you fail repeatedly? You really are failed fledglings, aren't you?"

The corridor they entered held a stench of chlorine and it opened out on a large swimming pool that at first glance had no other exit other than a door on the opposite side. Celeste pulled a face. "You cannot be serious."

"What?" Malcolm turned to look at his wife in confusion.

"I am not swimming through that," Celeste stated, with her arms crossed firmly.

Malcolm blinked. "You always bragged about how you were the league champion for your area in school and that you won all those medals."

"Which is all true," Celeste said, "but I'm not dipping a foot in that. It'll have some monster in it or else be filled with acid water or something."

He stared at the woman who had been so insistent that all three of their children become champion swimmers. She had been dragging them out of bed every morning at 4am to ensure that they got to practise, and if they didn't live up to her lofty expectations then they'd have to swim more punishing lengths after school. She also expected straight A* grades from all of them. Instead of considering that they might be putting too much pressure on their children, Malcolm found himself wondering if just maybe he and Celeste had put a little too much pressure on themselves to ensure that their children had the best of everything. The irony of this completely bypassed his brain.

He also found himself a little irritated that his wife was refusing to do something that was so obviously the correct course of action. Instead of getting into an argument with her however, Malcolm just took off his shoes, threw one into the pool and saw that all it did was merely float on the surface.

Carefully he lowered himself down into the water, hissing at the temperature change and anticipating some horrific death. After several moments he realised nothing else was happening. Taking a deep breath, he lurched forward into a simple breaststroke which, while not executed perfectly, was more than enough to get him across the twenty-five metres without a problem. Pulling himself up and out of the water, he shook himself off and turned back towards Celeste. "Come on, it's safe."

Celeste stared at the water in front of her. "There has got to be another way round."

Malcolm let out a sigh. He always got agitated when people did not follow the simple rules. "Celeste get in the water and swim for god's sake, the longer you stay there the more chance you have of being killed... again."

Celeste stamped her foot. "But this outfit is new."

"Sod the outfit, it's been ripped up and splattered in your blood. You can't even tell!" Malcolm pointed out. "Get over your high standards and get across here."

For a second Malcolm thought that the woman was just going to up and follow him without a question as she did take off her heels but then started whimpering. "I can't."

"It's a swimming pool, you were the champion!" Malcolm called out in exasperation.

"I just said that to give those brats some motivation!" Celeste screamed back. "I've never set foot in a pool in my life!"

Malcolm should have been shocked at that revelation, but he found himself not in the least bit surprised. He had never seen a single swimming award with Celeste's name on it, and had never even seen her take so much as a bath. She took showers because they were quicker and more convenient, and she wouldn't even dip her toe in the sea. Part of him felt a little bad for not having called her out on it earlier, but there had never seemed to be a reason to, so why bother?

Before he could think of a comeback though, he heard the distinctive sound of the growls from the dogs and felt his heart begin to hammer in his chest. "Celeste! Get in the pool and wade across now!"

"But-" she wailed back.

"The fucking dogs will eat you otherwise!" he shouted back, cutting her off, and knowing that he could not make it back across in time as there came the distinct sound of paws hitting the floor.

Celeste frowned and for some reason turned back to look down the corridor where the creatures were coming from.

Malcolm did not stick around to see what happened. The sounds of tearing flesh were more than enough to give him a hint and he charged forward with his heart beating rapidly. Maybe he could make it out alone, maybe that was better because if she wouldn't get into the water then what was the point of teaming up with the stupid woman in the first place? Sure, she was his wife, and he should be protecting her, but it was a dog eat dog world and he had to survive in any way he could.

Which is why, when the corridor presented three more tunnels to go down, he went straight forward figuring that it was the best solution to the problem that he had faced before. The corridor was pitch black and he thought that he heard a faint buzzing before he placed a foot on what felt like a metal plate. Which then buzzed before sending a lethal jolt of electricity straight through his system.

Silence.

A sharp intake of breath.

A high-pitched wailing sound

A freezing sensation.

"Haven't you figured anything out by now?" the girl standing at the beginning of the maze asked, her monotone voice holding a hint of disbelief. "I would have thought it would have been simple enough to figure out?"

"Go to Hell," Malcolm snapped, already pushing Celeste forward so that she wouldn't start arguing. "You don't know anything about us, bitch.

A deep chuckle came from the girl. "I am the Collector; I know everything about you both. I'm just surprised at how much you two don't know about each other."

Celeste sniffled. "I'm suing your arse when we get out of this mess."

"The dead cannot do such a thing. But do keep trying, this is highly amusing."

Neither Malcolm nor Celeste commented, simply continuing into the maze with the sole purpose of making it through just so that they could prove the little monster wrong. She was grating on their nerves, and it was clear that she had some kind of personal vendetta against them, so they were well within their rights to do something about it.

Once they got through the maze of course.

It barely took any time to reach the pool and Malcolm, being the forever helpful husband that he was, pushed Celeste into the water, got in himself, helped her to stand as it only came to roughly halfway up their bodies and pushed her out at the other end.

"Middle tunnel has electricity in it, so we're not going that way," he said, grabbing onto the woman's arm to haul her along as she seemed to be in some kind of trance after being in the water. There was a choice between left and right. Neither direction gave any clear indication of what lay beyond, which made sense, but it made choosing very hard.

Malcolm decided that they would head right, and they started down the tunnel which opened onto a room that looked like something out of a children's game show. There was a large grid set out with multiple circles that had to be stood on. On the opposite side stood a huge man in an executioner's cloak, hefting aloft an enormous axe that had the shiniest edge glistening off the pale lighting. Celeste seemed to come out of whatever stupor she was in and looked around. "It's a trap, there's no way we can cross."

"How do you know?" Malcolm asked, simply seeing the puzzle and nothing else.

Celeste glared at him, "There's no door on the other side, we'd just be stepping around in circles until he caught us."

Blinking, Malcolm looked towards the back wall and realised that it was just a black void which did not sit well with him at all. No obvious exit, no way through and clearly a trap designed to match his very unhealthy obsession with puzzles. He let out a sigh, taking several steps backwards with wary eyes watching for any sudden movements. The pair moved quickly back into the central hub and the man with the axe that was bigger than himself remained exactly where he was.

"Okay, we go left then," Celeste stated after a long release of breath.

Malcolm nodded, checked back down the tunnel they had come from just to make sure there were no dogs coming after them. Nothing. Maybe they only triggered if someone was stalling or left behind. That would make the most sense but then again most things in this place did not seem to follow any predictable pattern. Which was annoying him something rotten.

At least Celeste seemed to have calmed down now after her little fit, so that was something.

The corridor was the same as all the others but wound on for a much longer time. Both participants double checked every surface and bend with trepidation to ensure that they were not caught off guard again. Finally, they finished the loop only to come across a corridor with a large framed item covered with a billowing white sheet. Celeste blinked and looked back with concern. "Did we miss something?"

"No, I double checked everything," Malcolm said, which was true because he had very carefully examined the walls at regular intervals to make sure that there was not a door or a trigger lock or anything that would potentially kill them. Celeste would have joined in but could not ruin her expensive nails, despite them having already been broken or scuffed beyond repair.

Letting out a hum, Celeste checked around for any clues to indicate what they needed to do here as it was clear there was nowhere else to go. Carefully she stepped forward, taking hold of the sheet and gave it a pull. It fell away without a sound and crumpled onto the floor, revealing a mirror that merely reflected them both. Celeste frowned, turning to look towards her husband. "What is this?"

"No idea," Malcolm said, though he was already adjusting his tie and smoothing out his hair as if this was the perfect time to be grooming himself. Celeste was deliberately choosing to ignore the mirror except for stealing a quick glance. She did not want to see the ugly mess that she had become during their ordeal. She always looked perfect. She had to be perfect to survive the world that she found herself in. She had always demanded the same perfection of every woman in her life.

From what they had been through already, she knew that this was some kind of test and that they had to be smart to make it. She still couldn't understand why they were being forced to do this, it all seemed so unjust and unfair. She really wanted to kick some arses. Preferably the little brat at the front of the maze. She was always tearing down their attempts but giving them no other instructions about how to escape! She sounded almost impatient, as if this was somehow all their fault and that nothing they could do would ever match the expectations that she had of them.

An uncomfortable thought prodded lightly at the back of her head, but Celeste was quick to dismiss it as nothing more than an itch.

"Haven't you figured anything out yet?" she snapped instead, turning to look back at her husband whilst carelessly scratching at the back of her head.

"Hmmm?" Malcolm responded in the most unhelpful of manners, clearly still trying to sort out his damn appearance because he had gone into one of his bouts of perfectionism. Normally Celeste would be enraptured by this careful ritual that Malcolm would perform, ensuring that every last part of himself was pristine, neat, and perfectly groomed to a state of near orgasmic excellence. Malcolm wanted people to stare at him in complete and total awe because he looked like someone who could breeze into a room and solve all the problems in the world.

He looked like the kind of man who commanded respect from everyone in the room with just a perfected wave of his hand, the kind of man who was masculine and strong, who showed no emotions even in times of high stress. The kind of man that he imagined all the females desired and wanted to mate for the highest chance of producing the best offspring to fuel the reign of man for all eternity.

Right now, it was grating on Celeste's nerves and setting off a desire to scratch at herself constantly. "Have you figured out how we're supposed to get past this fucking mirror yet?"

"All in good time, my dear," Malcolm replied, seemingly unaware of his wife's irritation. "We cannot rush straight into-"

Celeste snapped and strode forward, slapping the man hard. "This isn't the time to be fussing and faffing over your fucking appearance, arsehole! If we don't move in the next few moments, we're going to be eaten by dogs again or had you fucking forgotten that we're in an endless maze of traps that are designed to kill us and send us back to the simpering whore at the front to be- This fucking itch! Make it stop!"

The woman was now scratching incessantly at her arms, legs, and anywhere else that she could reach with a series of grumbles and curses that were getting more annoyed by the second. Malcolm blinked, seeming to come back to their current situation.

He turned away from Celeste just for a moment to ground himself and found his eyes locking with his reflection in the mirror. Only it wasn't a reflection anymore. He saw himself as the perfect being he had always imagined himself to be but had never managed to become.

Celeste was in the reflection behind him, though there were hundreds of large, red ticks that were clearly biting through her skin and getting larger.

Carefully he turned and looked towards his wife, who was still desperately scratching at herself before looking at the opposite version of himself with a sinking feeling in the stomach. Only there was no reflection now, which caused him to step backwards in shock. Straight into the manly chest of his reflected self who towered above him with a killer smile etched on his face. "You were never the person you wanted to be. So instead, you deluded yourself into believing the lies you told yourself and then expected others to also believe, despite giving them no reason to."

Celeste was now screaming as she continued to scratch at herself, seemingly not noticing that she had broken the skin and was literally digging into herself and ripping huge, bloody chunks off her body.

"Just like she can't face the reality of her true thoughts because if she did they would eat her alive," the reflection said, chuckling in a way that Malcolm could not help but find incredibly attractive. After all, this was his perfect reflection. He wanted to slash at it, to just do something to prove that what it was saying about him was not true. Having to face this insecurity head-on was messing with his mind and making it so that he couldn't even think about what was going to happen next.

"You can't even deny it anymore, can you?" the reflection said. It was just so calm and perfect. "Or is your jealousy so all-consuming that you have to remain silent to save your own world from shattering?"

Malcolm glared towards the reflection and scoffed. "I am better than you."

"No, you're not, don't lie to yourself," the reflection said. Then, with a dull thump, it was clear that Celeste had fallen to the ground and was whimpering. Malcolm flicked his eyes over to her, grimacing as he saw her virtually destroyed body that was still trying to tear itself apart. He shuddered and looked back towards the reflection who cackled evilly at him. "You can't even bring yourself to care. You've both died so many times but you still can't see what is beyond the end of your nose, can you?"

About to argue, Malcolm instead found himself being pushed away by his reflection, crashing into the mirror which then shattered into a million pieces, sending him down into a void of all-consuming blackness. He could feel all his thoughts being ripped away and was left screaming in a place where no one and nothing could ever reach him.

Silence.

A sharp intake of breath.

A high-pitched wailing sound

A freezing sensation.

"Don't you say a fucking word," Malcolm snapped, pointing at the girl in the blue dress. "Or correction, you can start talking when you actually start explaining some things."

The Collector seemed to regard him with the same level of interest as someone who had just stood on a piece of sticky gum on the path and was trying to pull it off before it ruined their favourite shoes. "What do I need to explain? You have your task; you are the ones not completing it."

Malcolm stepped up straight in the girl's face. "You haven't warned us about any of the traps or told us how we're supposed to get through them yet are expecting us to tackle them flawlessly. How can you do that to someone? Huh? How can you expect perfection when you give nothing to indicate what that perfection should be?"

The Collector's jaw moved beneath the mask in such a way as Malcolm could imagine there was a smile creeping across her face. "Maybe you should reflect on those words for yourself, Malcolm."

Suddenly, Malcolm felt himself filled with unbidden rage. He pulled his fist back and proceeded to punch the Collector straight in the nose of her bicoloured cat mask, knocking her to the ground. The mask slipped, crashing down to the floor, and Malcolm promptly brought his foot up to kick her but missed as she pulled away from him with inhuman speed. The Collector rose, a thin, almost skeletal hand reaching out to cover her face, but Malcolm could see the pale, marred flesh, the slightest tinge of pink to her lips. Her eyes were no longer the swirling grey they had once been. Instead, one was a blazing red, glowing obscenely with anger and rage whilst the other was the deepest black that Malcolm had ever seen.

"You dare to..." The Collector's voice echoed with something ancient, a power that inspired both terror and utter devotion. Malcolm was terrified as he fell to his knees in front of her, wondering if he should be begging for her mercy or submitting to her will for the rest of eternity.

It did occur to him to wonder where his wife was, but he was a bit too preoccupied to really focus as the Collector was seething with rage and took several steps towards him. Malcolm feared that this would be his complete and total doom.

Suddenly from the ground the most beautiful blood-red and black rose sprouted. It grew quickly out of the ground, many thorned vines twisting around one another to form a figure that then burst forth in a flurry of black and red petals. Standing next to the Collector, embracing her, was a male figure, covered with a red robe and black chains. A skeletal mask covered the figure's face, looking something akin to a dog with very sharp canine teeth in a gleaming silver. Black fur highlighted with red cascaded from the top of the skull all the way down the back. "Hush now my love," the Beast said, his voice soft as the morning sunrise after a long harrowing night. "Don't give in to it. This one is not worth it."

The skull mask turned its hollow eyes towards Malcolm, who knew that he was being glared at. "Get your pathetic existence out of our face and away into the maze of your own pitiful creation."

Celeste grabbed the back of Malcolm's collar and hauled him back into the maze, where the dogs chased them as far as the first three-way junction. They were far more vicious than they had been before, their fur speckled with red and the largest, pale white eyes that either of them had ever seen. The largest, probably the alpha, watched them the longest before turning and trotting away. The couple could not help but feel if they made one wrong move the pack would return.

Celeste let out a long breath. "Let's get out of here, so we don't have to deal with her again."

Malcolm nodded and they proceeded down the corridor that led to the pool. This time Celeste did not argue about going in the water, despite still very obviously being afraid. Instead of going back down towards the mirror, they silently agreed to go right and try the puzzle room with the strange man. Surely it was the right way to go this time.

It took only a matter of thirteen moves for both of them to be carved up into little pieces by the man's huge axe.

Silence.

A sharp intake of breath.

A high-pitched wailing sound

A freezing sensation.

The Collector was not standing at the entrance waiting for them this time, the Beast however was, and he seemed to look down upon the pair of them with contempt before shaking his head.

"Not even the Devil himself would allow you two to pass onto redemption, you're both just such pathetic losers."

He pointed towards the start of the maze with a long finger, a sort of finality to the action that neither Malcolm nor Celeste could really ignore. Whatever hell they were in was clearly something that was not going to be escaped so easily. They had to have the resolve and willpower to get through this. Which they did have, because how else were they going to motivate their children to be the very fucking best at everything if they could not do it themselves.

The irony was completely lost on both of them, even after all the failures they had gone through.

Malcolm somehow found a little bit of courage within himself and rose his head sharply, sticking his nose up in the air with all the contempt that he could muster for this bizarre and detestable piece of excrement. "Once we are through this, you'll both be hearing from our lawyers."

The Beast snorted. "Dead men can't sue, you useless baby."

Celeste sneered, haughtily remarking, "You clearly know nothing of your situation then." She strode forward confidently, her high heels clicking as she moved. It was as though she were striding down a runway during her own private fashion show. "Come Malcolm, we'll prove this mutt wrong once and for all and then take him and his simpering little bitch to the cleaners."

For once, her husband was a bit more on the uptake as he rushed forward to almost drag her into the maze upon hearing the Beast growling out a warning that he was not to be trifled with.

They reached the first corridor easily, looking back to see that the ravenous dogs that had been constantly chasing them were now lounging almost casually next to the figure wearing the skull mask. They were receiving pets and treats as if they had done some kind of good job which was disgusting. The largest, however, was intently watching the entrance with its milk-white eyes glaring daggers. If they made one wrong move, it was clear they were going to be eaten alive.

Celeste let out a sigh. "Right, two steps, then count to five and take two larger steps, pause and count again."

"Let's do this," Malcolm said.

Together they took two steps forward, the first large blade swinging by their faces, and they counted to five. Then they took the two larger steps, balanced each other out and counted again. They repeated this eight times over until they were at the other end of the corridor without even the tiniest nick on them everywhere. They shared a smug little smile between themselves, before turning left and heading carefully down the next hall.

Malcolm suddenly scooped Celeste up in a bridal carry and said loudly, "I shall be your gallant knight!"

Celeste laughed as she playfully berated the man. "You should do this when we get to the water, you puzzle-solving genius."

"Nah, this is more fun," Malcolm said as he nimbly jumped from square to square, avoiding all the trap squares which would send an arrow flying straight towards them. He did so with gusto and flare, as if they hadn't been down this corridor countless times before. The man finished with a sickening prance of someone who expected their every achievement to be lauded and celebrated, no matter its insignificance.

Celeste laughed and applauded his show, as if they were somehow now in the perfect position and could easily waltz through this whole scenario without a care in the world. As if she believed when they escaped there would be a party waiting for them. She loved living in her own personal delusions about the world and how it worked. It made everything so much more amazing because her world was perfect and nothing bad ever happened to her because that was just the way that her fortunes had fallen.

She grabbed her husband's hand and they raced towards the swimming pool, giggling like high schoolers who had just graduated from the tyranny of a student life and were now ready to become roaring successes. Her face fell a little at the flash of light on the water, but she just batted her eyelashes at Malcolm. "Help me across, my grand knight?"

"Certainly, my lady," Malcolm said, hoisting Celeste onto his back as he easily waded across the water, laughing like they did not have a care in the world and were perfectly innocent of anything that had been brought up during the night. It was a strange moment, one that didn't feel connected to anything else, but they were both completely excited by power and had the world at their feet.

They were both laughing once they reached the other side, giggling like they had just shared an immature secret. Then they turned their smug, self-gratified eyes towards the three tunnels that led to nothing but death. "Hmm, I've just thought of something," Malcolm proclaimed loudly.

"Oh what, my most grand master of puzzles?" Celeste matched him in enthusiasm, even clapping her hands together eagerly, just short of lifting a heel to her bum and staring at her husband with large, longing eyes. It was such a cliche pose, but it seemed appropriate in the moment. Even though this was a man she had married for his wealth and would divorce in an instant if he gave her a reason.

"All these ways forward lead to nowhere, so the only way we can go is back to the start," Malcolm proudly stated, turning around to where the pool should have been. "Clearly the way forward is too difficult, so we should work our way backwards through things we've already tried successfully."

"Such an outstanding answer," Celeste replied, even if the logic was not that sound. However, there were sometimes things in this world that she did not understand, and her glorious husband was there to explain it anyway, so it wasn't like she was going to be misled to her death.

However, the pair's jolly demeanour faded away as they realised they were no longer looking at a pool but instead a new pathway with two roads leading off. One sloped downwards with a sign above it that read 'Noitpmeder' whilst the other led upwards with a sign that read 'Llehsihtniamer'.

Celeste made a face, "What non-English language is this gibberish?"

"I have no idea," Malcolm replied, tilting his head this way and that but then shrugging. "Explains why those two morons at the doors couldn't understand us anyway. They're just migrant scum who come to our great country to steal our hardworking boys' jobs."

For a second Celeste wanted to point out that one of them had been female and they had both spoken English very well, but she quickly dismissed that putrid thought from her mind. Either way they had to be inferior people from some loony place where manners and proper etiquette did not exist. "So which way do we go then, oh husband of mine?" she asked with an exorbitant amount of praise that would be sickening to the casual observer.

Malcolm pondered the two signs for a couple more seconds, before pointing to the one that went upwards. "They say to get out of any situation, you need to reach for the top and the only way is up after all."

"Oh, that is so true," Celeste said, taking hold of his arm to walk proudly next to her husband as they ascended out of this nightmarish place. She couldn't wait to hear the adoring crowds, see the congratulations banners being waved and the balloons cascading into the air whilst confetti descended in a glittering dance to the ground.

Only instead to be met with the harrowing silence of a dark, empty room.

The pair continued walking in the dark void, watching for anything that could possibly cause them further harm, as if this was a final trial for them to overcome. After a few moments of long silence, Celeste piped up, "What is going on? Why aren't we being rewarded like we were told that we would be for getting through the maze intact?"

Malcolm snorted. "I've no idea. Those two are rotten liars and we'll have sharp words with them once we find our way out of this blackness, I can tell you."

"You really expect a reward after that failure?" The Collector's voice rang out from behind the pair, and they turned sharply towards the sound.

She was sitting daintily with a cup of tea in the finest China set that either Malcolm or Celeste had ever seen. Her mask was back in place, slightly altered to allow her the chance to drink the sweet-smelling tea that steamed gently.

"Failure?" Celeste asked, confused. "We got through your pathetic little maze with our lives intact just like you said at the beginning."

"We didn't even take a single nick this time either," Malcolm chimed in.

The Collector looked up from her tea. "You took twenty-five minutes to complete the task I set."

"And?"

"It was easily doable in twenty," the Collector replied, clearly mocking Celeste's voice. "Even better, if you had concentrated it could have been done in fifteen minutes and set a new record."

Malcolm stepped forward, thrusting himself boldly in front of Celeste who looked horror-stricken. "You never said anything about a time limit! Just that we were losing time! You can't change the rules on a whim!"

"You're pathetic, only getting an A, when you could have gotten an A* if you had done just a little more work," came back a perfect replica of Malcolm's voice

Then more words filled the space. Everything sounded familiar and it dawned on the couple that these were all demeaning and cruel things they had said to their children in the past.

"You ought to have gotten an Outstanding report, not an Good report."

"I said that you were to make the swim team, not be on the second one."

"That task should have taken you ten minutes, you took twelve."

"So lazy, especially seeing as I granted you three hours sleep."

"What do you mean you choose drama? That is not acceptable. You will take sciences and ace them."

"You need to do ten more lengths, as you're three seconds down on your personal best."

"Why is this room a mess? You haven't scrubbed the carpets clean yet."

"I don't know what you mean by 'school trips', you are staying here, studying up for your final exams and not galivanting off to some poxy little park for the day."

"No boys, no drink, no sweets, no dates, no play dates, no books except those that you need to study and no pocket money until you reach all the goals that I have set for you."

"I won't hear of you going to any other school. I don't care, you will follow my orders and not argue with me as I am you're parent and you owe me for everything that I've done for you."

"The task was simple, how could you not do it properly the first time? Like it's not that hard to create an seven course feast is it?"

"That's not fair, you're twisting our words!" shouted Celeste, stomping her feet. "You're making us out to be the bad guys when all we did was provide the weaklings a perfect opportunity to prove themselves."

"Yeah, we gave support and encouragement every step of the way," Malcolm shouted in support of his wife.

The Collector stared at two supposed adults, almost confused by them. How the pair couldn't hear their own words properly and how they were still adamant that they were in the right. This was despite having taken more than ten thousand attempts to get through the death maze and they still had not taken the redemption choice. It had even been signposted with the word "Redemption" spelled backwards. Some people really couldn't see past their own noses, and it seemed like these two needed more of a lesson. Shaking her head, she sighed. "Still you are useless, spineless, cowards who cannot truly look at yourselves in the mirror and know what you did was wrong."

Before either adult in front of her could respond, the Collector raised her fingers in the air. "Clearly I need to send you back through another maze to get you two useless beings to understand."

SNAP!

Silence.

A sharp intake of breath.

A high-pitched wailing sound

A freezing sensation.

"It's a simple task," the Collector stated, watching as Malcolm and Celeste picked themselves up for the ten thousand and first time. "Get through the maze with your life intact and then you can return to the mortal realm."

The pair looked at her, lost and confused, before starting to demand answers which she had already given them time and time again. And again, they refused to listen. Her grey eyes drifted to the left, aware of a presence there that caused a dim smile to appear on her face as the dogs tore into the pair. "You shouldn't be here."

"Neither should you," came the soft reply.

"This is the path I choose," the Collector said back softly. "You can't change that."

"It wasn't your fault," the Beast retorted in his deep voice.

The Collector paused, letting out a sigh. "I still did what I did."

"You were surviving. The only way you knew how."

"Go back to your duties," the Collector said. "I do not wish to talk any further."

There was a long pause and the Collector found herself for a moment, just a moment, standing in a field surrounded by wheat and hay with blood dripping from her fingers. Tears fell from her eyes. "Why weren't you here earlier? Why did you leave us so long? I wouldn't have done this if I had known... Why? Why? Why?"

Silence.

Followed by a sharp intake of breath

A high-pitched wailing sound

A freezing sensation.

The pair in front of her were terrified but going through the same motions as before. The Collector sighed before turning to step away.

Some souls were worth it, these two perfectionists were not.

UNDER THE BED

Charlie always preferred the dark.

The shadows embraced her. They kept her warm and safe on the silent nights when nothing would creep around the doors. Then the Lights would spill through the cracks, filling up the edges of the frames and banishing the shadows to the farthest corners where they could not help her.

The Lights were falsely soothing. They promised many sweet things, speaking in soft tones that were captivating and joyous. Candy-coated words, dashed with sprinkles and ice cream that were meant to make all the horrible nightmares go away. Because the Lights were there to protect, the Lights were there to love, the Lights were what kept Charlie from being consumed by things that were not hers to understand.

As long as she remained silent. Still.

Perfect.

Beautiful.

Innocent.

But Charlie had learnt that the Lights were worse than the shadows, that the Lights brought about figures that were tall and pale. With hungry eyes, smirks that were supposed to look sweet and charming but were laced with malicious intent. The Lights brought about feelings that were terrible. Sensations that were barely understandable. And pain.

Affliction.

Strain.

Distress.

It was not a surprise to find Charlie lying on her bed, in the total darkness on a rainy night just listening for the sounds. Those sounds were indicators that the Lights were approaching. Some Lights did not hide their approach. They were bold and brash, making it known that they were on their way with sweets and lollipops. They would expect smiles and silence in return whilst they played. Others tried to sneak, as if they were some kind of elusive predators that were bearing down on the prey that was waiting for them. Occasionally there would be a Light that would be almost silent, nervous maybe, as if they were aware that this was terribly wrong and downright disgusting.

They never stayed that way for long.

Tonight though, there was just the pitter-patter of rain on the window which Charlie had not looked out of for many years. In fact, she wasn't even sure if there was a view out of that window to begin with. When she had been put in here, she had been too small to see out of it and then the Lights had boarded it up so by the time she grew up to be tall enough to see out it did not matter.

Sometimes she wondered if anyone was looking for her. If anyone missed her. If the drinks that she was given at the end of the Lights' visits were indeed just something to help her sleep or something to make her forget. She had stopped finishing her drinks over the last few visits, feeling strange each time she did. However, Charlie would also feel better because she began to focus on things that weren't just the Lights. The passage of time, the noise of the rain on the glass, how there was a small hatch underneath the bed.

It led nowhere; it was just a small hole in the floor used for storage but Charlie sometimes pretended that it was a gateway to something. A place where the Lights could not reach her. A place where the pain would stop. A place that would eventually help her get free.

There was a device in the small hole. One of the Lights had left it last time they came for their game and because she had only drunk half of her special drink, Charlie had been able to hide it away. Whether the Light noticed or not, she had no idea because it never returned and that had been... how long ago?

Charlie did not know. Everything was the same down here. The darkness and the shadows were her only friends. Though the vague memory of an abstract thought that time existed in forms other than the darkness and the Lights, did sometimes poke at her mind but was always dismissed. Time did not matter in how long it passed. There was only keeping the darkness close and the Lights away.

However, as the rain continued, Charlie realised that there had not been a visit from any Light for a while. Not even the one who regularly would drop off a tin of food and a cup of water.

That was odd. It broke the pattern.

Charlie raised herself up on her bed, body stiff and uncooperative with the lack of movement and the sores on her back and buttocks. Carefully she swung her bare feet over the edge of the bed that she was forced to stay on, barely registering the temperature of the wood as it scratched at her feet. Something was different. There was a new echo to the ever present sound of silence and it took Charlie a long while to realise that there were no creaks coming from up above her head. The shadows up there were some of the deepest and darkest, rarely opting to come down to comfort her. However, Charlie had always attributed that to the fact that they were holding up whatever ceiling was above her.

Blinking, she turned her head up towards the darkest shadows, not noticing anything different except the lack of noise. She figured that she was in an underground room though whether she was under a house or something else, Charlie did not know. By now, the Lights would be moving around, going about whatever it was that they did before coming to see their silent, perfect being with whom they could do as they pleased.

It was silent.

Echoing.

Constant.

Breath-taking.

Spinning back towards the bed, Charlie whispered, "What are you doing there?"

Sitting on the covers, hind legs down, front legs straight, black red fur spilling out in all directions, with brilliant, white teeth and glowing, deep-yellow eyes was The Beast. A creature that Charlie had no reason to believe was real but knew instinctively was protecting her every time it turned up. "The Lights will be here soon," she continued in a tiny whisper. "They don't like you much."

The big head tilted to the side, sort of resembling a very large dog or a wolf but one that had come from the realm of nightmares. If the creature was bothered by such a statement, then it showed no outward signs. Instead, its burning eyes were focused directly on the door as if it were waiting for something. Charlie blinked, unsure as to what to do anymore. Usually, the shadows that manifested would only do so for a short length of time and then disappear when she told them to. Quite why they would, Charlie did not know but there was something different about this one.

All the other shadows had basically looked like shadows. Just formless blobs with the occasional illuminated eyes that usually indicated that there was something else there. This one had form, colour and teeth.

Teeth were new.

Before Charlie could whisper another wish for the Beast to disappear, there came a sound from the door which made her spin sharply. There was a sliver of yellow light from around the edges. However, unlike the Lights which would normally appear with a constant, warming presence that allowed her to adjust a little bit to them before they came into the shadowy room, this one was blinding. It flashed about, as if moving rapidly and seemed to be incapable of staying still for more than a second.

Charlie covered her eyes with her arms, fighting back the instinct to start sobbing. The Lights did not like her sobbing or making any noise in the slightest though she never understood why.

"Go away," she whispered, though whether to the strange Light which was frantically moving around the door or else the Beast on the bed, Charlie could not say.

All she knew at that moment was that there was something wrong. Something about this situation that just did not sit well in her stomach. Nothing usually sat well in it to begin with, but tonight everything just felt off.

Wrong.

Trembling.

Unfinished.

That last thought had her scurrying back to the bed where she tried to clamber up onto the hard mattress to cover herself with the threadbare blanket, but the Beast was still sitting there. It had not moved a single inch in the time that she had been watching this new Light. It did not even move when she whisper-yelled at it, nor when she reached forward to attempt to weakly push it away.

She knew that it was a lost cause because it was only a mere shadow, but the touch of a human normally drove the shadows away. Even her stick-thin arms that shivered and broke easily with the way that some of the Lights liked to play their games, would normally be more than enough to make the shadows retreat, not to be seen again until everything was over. Then she would be alone with the silence, and it was just another waiting game for the Lights to come back for whatever they wanted next.

But this time, her fingers touched something. It wasn't smooth like velvet, or rough like rope. It felt as soft as a cloud, yet densely matted together. It was warm, welcoming, and made her just want to curl up next to this large beast and never have to face the Lights ever again.

She pulled back with a little gasp, not quite daring to believe the thought that had just crossed her mind at that moment because the Lights gave her everything she needed to survive. They only asked for her silence in return when they...

Again, Charlie fought back the urge to sob, because she realised that for the longest time, she had preferred the shadows. She would prefer the Lights not knowing she existed. She would prefer being forgotten about in this dark room where only the rain pattered against the boarded-up window and the darkness would greet her tired eyes whether she opened them or not. Charlie wanted nothing more than for the Lights to go away forever, to never come back and to never seek her out again. She wanted to be left alone yet cuddled and protected but not have to pay anything for getting those things.

Charlie did not understand many things in life, how this had all started and why they expected her to do such things when she barely even knew what she wanted anymore. A headache started to pound inside her mind, making her whimper and finally release the sob that she had been holding back for years because she did not know what anything meant anymore.

A low grumble caught her attention and Charlie looked up to see the Beast now lying on the bed, his expression – she chose to assume that it was a male creature even though she had no reasoning as to why – soft and understanding. The Beast did not speak words, but Charlie understood that gaze, the offer that was being made towards her and for the first time in an unknowable length of time, Charlie felt as though there was someone there for just her. Someone who would hold her, someone who would reassure her and most of all protect her.

She sobbed louder and rushed at the Beast, clinging to his strange fur that smelt of burnt out fires and the remains of over-prepared food. She found only comfort in those smells, the scents of a world away from this dark room, where there was only the foul stench of sweat, the bodily fluids that sometimes the Lights left behind and that acid-sweet smell of the drink they gave her. They said it tasted of bubble gum and candyfloss but it was more like the bitterest lemons mixed with vinegar. Charlie sobbed into the red black fur, clinging and pulling at the Beast who simply remained on the bed completely unbothered by her actions.

The Light continued to flicker frantically around the door, muffled shouting coming from it, but Charlie paid it no real heed. There were always sounds before the Lights appeared, mostly they sounded quite jolly. Right now, it did not sound like that.

Panic.

Fright.

Anger.

After a long while, Charlie's sobbing stopped, and she instead just leant heavily against the Beast. A sort of smile crossed the ragged lips before a long, slimy, bright pink tongue licked against her face. Charlie sighed in relief, feeling as though she had been cleaned properly for the first time since arriving at this strange, dark place with only shadows for friends.

Briefly Charlie turned her attention back to the place where the Light had been flitting about in a frantic state. It took her a moment to fully see the area, as the Beast had decided to lick her face again before going on to comb his tongue across other parts of her body that were not covered by the flimsy grey nightgown that they had given her. Finally, her eyes focused enough to see that the Light was still far too bright, sharp and piercing. However, it had stopped its frantic movement. It was hovering near the left side of the door, almost as if it were debating whether to enter, which was concerning.

The Lights did not wait for anything after the sounds of joy disappeared, in fact the lack of those happy noises was disturbing to Charlie. She couldn't remember the Lights ever being that quiet and that uneasy feeling in her stomach crept back tenfold on what it had been before.

Scrape.

Scratch.

Click.

The door to the room opened.

The Light shone directly into Charlie's eyes, blinding her which automatically caused a yell to tumble unbidden between her lips. Making a noise was a bad thing. It would bring the Lights' anger, make them hit harder, make them do nastier things and there would certainly be no more sweet treats. Charlie was meant to be their perfect, beautiful, quiet doll who would never say a word to any of them.

Even when it hurt. Even when she did not want to play. Even when she threw up their gifts to her, because if she made a sound, then the worse things would happen. Charlie had only once ever been on the receiving end of one of those; it was the reason that they had to give her the special drinks in the first place. To stop her from screaming and freaking out every time she recalled it.

Now she couldn't even remember the details, but the emotions lingered and the barest mention was usually enough to send her into an noisy panic attack. Which the Lights hated.

Silent.

Perfect.

Peaceful.

Stomping boots approached her and the piercing light got closer. It burned through her tightly closed eyelids even as she tried her very best to will it all away. She feared for the remains of her new shadow friend that would be banished, even more so than she feared what the Light was going to do to her for making a sound.

She could survive whatever they were going to throw at her, her new friend the shadow beast was going to be sent back to the place that it came from, and it would probably not return. She was not worth his time. Charlie was not worth anyone's time. She was just a servant to the will of the Lights, and nothing could ever change that fact.

An enormous hand landed on her arm, ripping it away from her face to cause more of the piercing, luminescent, white light to assault her already aching eyeballs. "Fucking squawking bitch! Shut the fuck up with your crying and snivelling." A voice she recognised as one of the Lights that occasionally came in to 'clean her up', and who in her own mind she referred to as 'Cleaning Light', snapped harshly at her. No care or compassion, no understanding or attempts to soothe a very distressed child in a terrifying situation. "You'll bring the upper bosses down on your head and they'll play with you harder than we do."

Charlie tried to hold back her sobbing like she always could do in the past, but something had changed. Cleaning Light was fearful, panicked and not his usual self which made Charlie believe that the upper bosses were already coming down on them. She couldn't hold back a sob and tried to pull her arm away from the hand that was tightening more than enough to cause bruises that would last well after their encounter was over.

"Don't you fucking dare start to disrespect me, you little shit," Cleaning Light snapped, this time yanking her arm forward as he stepped backwards, away from the bed. "We have to get fucking moving and you behaving like a sack of terrified shit is not–"

Whatever the end of that sentence was going to be, it never came to be spoken aloud. Instead, there came a simple snap of heavy jaws followed by the sound of wet meat hitting the floor. Charlie pried her tear-filled eyes open to see Cleaning Light staring in shock towards the place where his arm had been attached to his body just a moment before.

The Beast's white teeth were now splattered with blood and a fearsome growl escaped from his throat.

Gasp.

Crunch.

Splosh.

The body slumped to the floor and the piercing light clattered away to the corner of the room where it landed at an angle that lit up the entire scene. Charlie stared at what had formerly been Cleaning Light, who was now missing an arm, and most of his face accompanied with large claw marks down his chest from gullet to groin.

Red stuff was pooling silently around the body, seeping into the fur of the monster who merely snorted in disgust before stepping away. He turned to look at Charlie, his eyes cold and deadly to all but her. The offer still stood.

Nodding silently, Charlie reached out towards the creature's fur again and then climbed up onto his back. The Beast paused long enough to spit at the former Cleaning Light before padding his way out of the strange, dark room.

The corridor they emerged into was a dark grey and reminded Charlie of the walls in the room in which she had previously been held. The air here was strange, almost dusty, but with an extra heaviness to it which the young girl could not place. The Beast, whom she was riding, strode forward with a grim confidence that seemed to ooze out of his fur. He did not seem to be afraid of anything.

Charlie wondered why he had come to get her and then suddenly remembered the device in the little recess. Gently she pulled on the ear of the Beast, who stopped to tilt his head towards her in question. The yellow eyes softened slightly, ready to listen and understand. "One of them left something, I hid it," Charlie whispered, getting down off the Beast's back and heading back into the room where the shadows had tried to keep her safe for however many years that she had been kept there.

The body of the Light was still there, still oozing out the red stuff that seeped into the cracks in the panels and stained the wood a completely different colour. Charlie made her way past the growing pool, stepping carefully so as to not leave a trail herself and ducked under the bed to remove the tile. The device was sitting where she had left it, the screen blank but her little fingers closed around it in seconds.

Bang!

Bang!

Whimper.

Charlie threw her hands over her ears, trying desperately not to scream as the gunshots echoed around the small, enclosed space. Her ears rang with the sound, drowning out everything else as her heart pounded. Another volley of shots came, accompanied by a quick succession of small, orange flashes that forced the young girl to close her eyes. Desperately she tried to focus on her heartbeat, to seek comfort and solace in the shadows that had always kept her safe but there were none of the ones that she recognised. Driven away by Cleaning Light's glow that cut harshly into every corner and made it impossible for them to reach her.

She started shivering where she lay, desperate to hear any sounds other than the high-pitched ringing or the thunderous thumping of her heartbeat.

"Motherfucker," a voice cut through the noise, disbelief and shock radiating from it as another of the Lights stepped into the room.

"Is that thing dead?" called a distant voice, probably coming from the corridor.

"No, but Burrows is," the first voice called back, sounding as though they couldn't quite believe what it was that they were looking at. "Shit, half of his face is missing."

There was a startled shriek followed by another bang. "Whose fucking mutt is this anyway?"

"I've no idea, never seen it before," replied the Light who was not Burrows. "Just make sure that it's dead because fucking Christ, what it's done to Burrows! I don't want that to happen to me."

Another shot, this one slightly muffled. "Whatever man, grab the bitch and let's get the fuck out of here before the pigs come looking for any more trouble."

Charlie tried her best to push herself further under the bed but let out a scream when her leg was grabbed, and she was hauled out. Another Light was streaming right into her eyes, blinding her from the rest of the lit up room and causing tears to flow freely down her face. She was shaken harshly. "Shut up, bitch, we're getting out of here and we can't if you keep making noise."

Charlie wouldn't listen and deliberately made more noise, wriggling backwards as harshly as she could before attempting to kick the man in the face. Her heel connected with his nose, hard enough to bruise and more than enough to shock the man who let out a yelp and dropped her to the ground. Charlie ran as fast as her legs would carry her, straight out into the corridor only to find a gun pointed directly at her face.

Fear.

Terror.

Obedience.

"That's quite enough from you, little worthless cunt," said the new Light who was staring her down with an angry look in his eyes. There were already several marks on his face, ones that looked like they had been inflicted from a fight and his knuckles were busted open in an ugly mess. "You're coming with us right now."

A hand latched onto the back of Charlie's flimsy nightdress to start hauling her up the stairs. "Fuckfaced little twat. I'll teach you a lesson for breaking my nose."

"Ha, that'll be the least of your worries, mate," said the gun wielder before turning to head up the stairs.

Charlie felt the urge to start shouting again, to start screaming and causing a fuss because maybe it would attract the attention of someone. Someone who was not a Light, someone who would come to her aid and make sure that she was safe and would be looked after forever. Or maybe part of her dreamt of the relief that she would be granted if she made a big enough fuss and a lot of noise that they would take her out. End the misery that she had been subjected to, the constant silence, the constant games that made no sense to her and rewarded her with nothing.

Because what did she really have to lose? She had nowhere to go. She didn't know of anyone who was searching for her. Surely, if anyone was, then someone would have come and gotten her by now, right?

Just as she was about to open her mouth, however, something flickered in the shadows. A form was building up, growing bigger and seeming to seethe with an anger that forced her mouth to instantly close. Though not from fear for herself, but the knowledge that in the next few seconds the Lights dragging her up the stairs would be the least of her worries.

The door at the top of the stairs suddenly slammed shut.

"Shit! What the fuck!" yelled the Light with the gun who immediately ran up to grab the handle. "Why is it locked?"

"Just yell for Harkins on the other side," came the disgruntled voice of the Light who was holding onto Charlie. "The idiot probably just let it swing closed because he's getting off to those pictures again, the creepy fucker."

The first Light started calling out, rattling the door handle that was firmly stuck in place. Charlie still watched the darkness below, recognising the Beast that was now stalking silently towards the two Lights, his large paws nearly covering two steps at a time. The back of Charlie's dress was released and she silently scuttled to the nearest wall, shaking with the knowledge that she was going to be the witness to something gory.

The Beast stopped whilst the two Lights were still yelling their heads off. He was several steps below them and turned his large head to look at Charlie. The red eyes held all the thoughts that were running around the creature's head, the intent to brutally kill these two but also the need to protect the little girl that was shivering in front of him. His stare was calculating, as if he were solving a complex problem that required a lot of thought.

Then his eyes rose up to the top of the door, where there was a half-circle window, misted over by such a thick layer of dirt and grime that it was next to impossible to see it unless one was actively looking for it.

Seeming to come to a decision, the Beast tilted his head in such a manner as if to indicate to Charlie that she was to come closer. The girl glanced at the two frantically yelling Lights, that were half-shrouded in their own self-created darkness. They were completely distracted and seemed to have almost forgotten about her. Keeping low, Charlie hugged the wall until she was a couple of steps away before rushing straight to the warm fur that felt like the safest place to be in the world at that moment. A gentle rumbling growl came from the much larger creature, as if trying to sooth her in the best way it could before the long snout gently nudged Charlie into standing straight in front of his huge head.

Instinct made her turn to present her back to the Beast, only slightly jumping when she heard the shouts of, "Where the fuck are you going, you little bitch?" from one of the very pissed off and angry Lights further up the stairs. Charlie cast her eyes upwards, seeing the two Lights looking at her in confusion as if they could not understand how she had just gotten down behind them. This was despite neither of them paying the least bit of attention to her, but she did not speak a word.

The large, white teeth ever so gently took hold of the back of her night gown and slowly started to lift her up. From the expression on the two Lights' faces as she rose up, they clearly could not see the Beast behind her that was due to devour them in a matter of seconds. Their minds were confused and haunted by the sight of a little girl, with a thin body and a sunken expression rising up into the air as if she were possessed by some devil that was coming to reign uttermost terror onto them both.

For the first time in a very long time, a smile crossed Charlie's face. Wicked, cruel and filled with all the nasty thoughts that she had allowed herself from time to time in order to survive. The thoughts of what she would do to the Lights should the opportunity ever present itself. What if one were to leave behind a sharp, pointy thing that she could use to drive into their flesh? Or perhaps if she could get free of the restraints long enough to chain them to the bed? Then she could drive all the instruments that they used on her into their bodies to see how much they enjoyed it. The press of a wet nose on the back of her neck told her that the Beast did not quite approve of those thoughts and Charlie figured that he would be dealing back that revenge for her, so she allowed the thoughts to fall away. However, the smile still lingered on her face at the thought of what awaited two frozen Lights.

She desperately wanted to speak or say something to them but chose to keep her silence just in case one of them survived.

The window came into view and Charlie reached out her hand, barely worried about the grime that covered the window. She was covered in much worse. Her hand connected with the glass, which felt cool on her palm. As she pushed against the window it opened with a very heavy, screeching groan. A breeze brushed across her cheeks and Charlie revelled in it. A black red, furry paw pushed past her, fully opening the window and helping Charlie scramble through the gap before gently lowering her down to the ground on the opposite side of the door.

Harkins, the one who was supposed to be watching this side of the door, was trembling so violently and the gun in his hand was shaking so much that there was no way he would be able to make an accurate shot. Charlie felt her feet touch the floor before a rush of fur engulfed her vision as the Beast extended his head out towards Hawkins.

Snap.

Squelch.

Thump.

The fur cleared away from Charlie's vision as the Beast retreated through the window it had just come through, leaving the girl on the opposite side of the door.

Her eyes took in the sight of the headless body in front of her, but she felt nothing for the man. If he was part of the Lights, then he was one that she had not personally met but that didn't mean that he hadn't done terrible things to others like her. She looked around the room that she was in, seeing that it was like some form of reception, but it was still enclosed. The floor was tiled, making it weirdly cold on her bare feet and the walls had been decorated with the vilest looking shade of yellow wood panelling that it made her feel uneasy. Or maybe it had just been stained with all the cigarette and cigar smoke. The Lights all seemed to be prolific smokers. Or perhaps this was where they filled the strange, glass vials that contained the disgusting smells that would constantly give her headaches and made her see things she never wanted to witness again.

Charlie took a few steps towards the body, kneeling to claim the gun for herself as even though she wasn't completely sure how to use it, she figured that it may be a good idea to have something in case she got separated from the Beast again. She did notice that the man's head was missing and when she thought back about the others that had been attacked, they too were missing their heads. If they were not missing, then at the very least something had tried to remove them. However, now was not the time to dwell on missing heads she decided, as she stood up and walked towards the desk. There were a few rather plush looking couches that were also stained with the horrible nicotine stuff, as well as a pot plant that looked a very startling shade of green. She paused next to it, reaching out a curious hand only to feel a cold plastic which made sense.

Wherever this room was, no one was supposed to really spend any time here.

She headed towards the desk again, seeing a computer which was powered down, a stack of papers that she couldn't read but the main thing that she was interested in was the black phone sitting there. Some vague memory called forth the idea that if ever she were in trouble, she could lift the receiver and press the bottom right hand key three times, and it would connect to people who would help. Part of her thought that the device which had been under the bed would have done the exact same thing but she had no idea how to turn it on let alone use it so this would probably be the more sensible option.

Walking around the desk, Charlie pulled herself up onto the chair that moved a little bit before she settled down onto it. It was surprisingly comfy despite being a little on the big side and Charlie marvelled at the sensation for a second. Her eyes were drawn to the opposite side of the door where just faintly came the sound of crunches, scratches, and lots of munching. Strangely she felt nothing that made her feel uneasy and instead just focused on picking up the phone. It felt strangely heavy in her hands and very unreal despite it being just there.

Click.

Silence.

Dial tone.

"Which emergency service do you require?" came a sudden unexpected voice and Charlie squeaked, dropping the receiver in surprise. It clattered down to the ground, the hollow thudding noise echoing in the silent room surrounding her.

There was an exceptionally long pause, or at least it felt like that to Charlie, before the voice spoke again. "Which emergency service do you require?"

Cautiously stepping down off the chair, the girl took the receiver back into her hands and brought it up towards her ear. The voice was repeating the question again, sounding almost robotic but with an edge that suggested that it was going to go away soon because she had not spoken.

"Help," Charlie whispered.

Another pause.

"Which emergency service do you require?"

"Help me," Charlie continued to whisper, instinctively hiding under the desk that she was next to as the sounds from before had gotten eerily silent.

The pause was more thoughtful now. "Do you need assistance?"

"Help," Charlie spoke back, turning her head towards the door which was creaking open softly. From the restricted view she could only see a pair of heavy, leather-booted feet. Shivers began to run through her body as they started to step directly towards her and through the tears welling up in her eyes, she swore that she could see a pile of fur on top of one of the Lights. "The Light is coming for me. He's going to lock me away again, bring other Lights to do things to me. Help me, please help me!"

Charlie's voice rose with each word, the taste of freedom that she had momentarily been feeling completely draining away as those heavy boots kept coming towards her in a steady fashion. Part of her knew that it was probably better to stay still and silent, as the Light's anger was bound to be ruthless after all that had happened on this strange night. She was giving her position away but what other choice did she have? Her chance had probably long gone by now and even if the person speaking on the other end of the line could send help to her, everything would be in vain.

This was the night that she was going to die, Charlie was certain of it. Though she did not know if she preferred death or living more right at this moment in time.

The boots rounded to her side of the desk and the young girl looked up, blinking her lost eyes towards the figure. No scream came from her lips as she had initially expected because the man standing before her now, was not a Light. He appeared tall, with a thin build that was more skeletal than human, but he wore a dark red robe lined with ancient symbols in gold. The fabric looked old and worn, almost as if he had climbed out of a grave with the amount of dust and grime clinging to it. Adorning his head was the face of the Beast, long strands of black red fur heading down the length of his back and the same solemn but recognisable yellow eyes shone out towards her. Charlie blinked in confusion but held the receiver out towards the man as he beckoned for it, kneeling next to her with a hand extended out.

"Police, Detective Spooner." A voice that was heavy, deep, and sounded like it came from the underworld itself came out of the man-creature in front of the little girl, but no fear clung to her now. His tone reminded her of the soft, comforting grumbles that the Beast let out, the ones that were meant to comfort and protect. It was soothing and welcome. Charlie instantly trusted this figure who never took his eyes off her whilst relaying information over the phone. She barely registered the words he was saying, feeling tired, heavy and confused all at once but also knowing instinctively that at this moment in time she was safe.

After a little while, the Beast replaced the receiver onto the phone and Charlie found herself immediately gathered into the protective arms. Whilst she registered the frailty of this man, she still felt safe and protected. It was easy to imagine that she was being wrapped up in the warmest of blankets, carried after a long sunny day by someone who loved her. She would be tucked up safely in bed by those same hands before the Beast under the bed would come out to protect her through the night and drive away anything that threatened to cause her harm. These were the arms of someone who would chase away the nightmares, lift her up high just to make her laugh and guide her when she was unsure of where to go. Charlie never wanted to be away from this feeling ever again, even though in her head she knew that they would have to be parted at some point. "Let's get you out of here," the deep, rumbling tone said, and the little girl nodded tiredly.

She felt herself being picked up by those thin, protective arms and heard the rhythmic steps that the man took to head out of the building. It was soothing and calming to her frazzled nerves which had been through so much tonight, and the soft sound began to lull her into a sleep that had been a very long time coming.

Step.

Step.

Ste- scrunch.

Charlie opened her eyes sharply as the Beast came to an abrupt halt, straightening his back and snarling at a figure standing in front of them, with waves of anger radiating from him.

Standing in an adjoining doorway (Charlie was now firmly under the impression that this place was just made entirely of doors) was another man. Though this one immediately drove fear into her heart.

Father Jahiem Glaz held the biggest smirk on his face. The lines of his face seemed exaggerated, almost as though the smirk didn't belong to him at all, but that he had stolen it from someone else and stretched it over his own bones. He was huge in both directions, with a gut that wobbled alarmingly every time he moved and more stretch marks than should have been considered healthy on any exposed pieces of his skin. The smirk widened, revealing the rows of perfectly, almost luminescent, white teeth that he had sharpened over the years in service to something that Charlie did not understand. He looked like a shark, who had gorged too many times on the flesh of sinners who came to confession and never returned. On the surface world, he was revered and renowned for combining his belief with scientific breakthroughs but down here, he was an overlord who took the greatest pleasure in destroying innocence and mocking it with brutality that was legendary.

It was Father Glaz who had introduced Charlie to the Lights, or more rightly dragged her kicking and screaming into their domain, telling them that she was ripe for conception of the newest heavenly arrival. Charlie had never understood a word of what the man was saying or how he could even believe the nonsense that he spouted, but she understood that he was terrifyingly deadly when it came to his plans being interrupted.

"Well, well, well," Father Glaz spoke with a thick clawing accent, vaguely Germanic but mixed with Nordic influences that was clotted with grease and smoothed over with practised ease to make many fall under his spell. "If it isn't the failure."

Charlie glanced up at the Beast, noting that his yellow eyes were narrowed in anger and distaste towards Glaz, but he did not speak a word to the man. Father Glaz chuckled however, seeming to have expected this. "Did you really think your actions would go unnoticed? Stupid boy, you should have taken the opportunity to flee when you had the chance to do so. Now you're just caught in a constant cycle of murder, betrayal and self-flagellation because you cannot undo the mistakes of your past and reach the ever glowing beauty of the world anew."

A snort came from the Beast. "You talk too much, for a dead man."

"That's a funny one," Father Glaz replied, pulling out a gun which had a series of intricate engravings upon it. "Seeing as you have no way to reach me in time with that little bitch in your hands."

Flicking a switch which caused several glowing, red lines to appear on the gun and work their way towards the barrel, Father Glaz's eyes glimmered with a malice that not even Charlie had seen before. "Time to send you back to hell, you little shitbag."

Bang!

Bang!

Bang!

Charlie tumbled to the floor, barely letting out a noise as she instinctively rolled away and hid behind the nearest piece of furniture. Carefully she peeked out, only allowing her soft, brown eyes to show.

Smoke coiled up from Father Glaz's gun, the smirk he had been wearing slowly slipping down from his over-stretched face into a frown as he stared. The Beast was still standing, his right hand out in front of him with a gaping bullet hole directly through the centre of it. Blood dripped down in small little droplets through the centre.

Father Glaz flinched, clearly surprised, and confused but realised that the Beast in front of him was not just going to give up that easily.

The Beast took a step forward, sharp, white teeth showing through the blackness of his fur. The man raised up his gun once again, firing it in rapid succession. Some completely missed the mark, one tore through the shoulder of the Beast but he kept up his steady pace. A final bullet slammed into the creature's stomach before exploding with a burst of purple and blue smoke that emitted a bloodcurdling scream from the very bottom of the universe. For a second there appeared to be something very long, slimy and wriggling coming out of the Beast's body, as if he were being forced to bring something into the world that should never have been summoned.

The Beast snarled straight back, grabbed the tentacles, and ripped them straight out of the portal, revealing a small brightly coloured squid-like monster. His free hand slashed through the portal like a hot knife through butter which shattered almost instantly into hundreds of painful shards. The small squid-like thing screeched in retaliation and spat a thick, black ink towards the Beast's face.

At such close range, there was no way the shot could miss and the Beast dropped the squid, staggering backwards for a few seconds with a constant burning and hissing coming from the wounds. Father Glaz smirked as the squid-like creature ambled up to him before clambering up to sit neatly on the side of his head with angry eyes directed towards the Beast. "Ha, you really think that I wouldn't ensure that I got something that could deal with the likes of you on my side? You're just as slow and pathetic as when this all went down."

The man was letting the power go to his head, Charlie realised, drunk off the satisfaction that he thought that he had the upper hand and that he held victory within his grasp. Worried, she glanced towards the Beast, who was half on the floor, barely moving. It was as if the effects of the poison might be the end of him. Charlie reminded herself of earlier. She had to have faith that he'd come back. That the Beast wasn't that easy to take down and that Father Glaz was in for a rude awakening very shortly.

Father Glaz, however, seemed more inclined to just keep taunting the Beast in his prone position on the floor. "Though it is interesting that you are the one who is still alive. Or more correctly, living whatever the fuck you call this zombie-induced existence. I would have put my money on that pretty little bitch of yours. I would have loved to seen your face as we caught up with her and those fucking brats. She squealed like the little freak that she was."

He laughed aloud at his own joke, barely looking at the Beast below him who had stopped moving but was listening to each and every word. "But I bet you made her squeal more; bet you got off on it all the time when you were fucking her cause that's what you did? Only way to get all those pretty little sons of bitches out of her right? Why you never wanted to keep her in the safety of our home I do not know. It would have made everything so much easier as it would have opened the gates of Heaven for you rather than the Hell that you face yourself with now, you useless little-"

Father Glaz looked towards the Beast for the first time during his little rant and stuttered his long winded speech to a complete halt.

Standing fully upright with not a single mark on him from the poison or the gaping hole that had been forced through his hands was the Beast. The black dog-like mask glimmering with golden sigil's that contrasted with the red-black fur that still cascaded down his back in glistening rolls. The Beast looked like he had just been newly awakened, stepping out of a portal to Hell and nightmares, and would never stop coming for those he had the right to claim. The Beast just stood there, with blazing, red eyes boring straight into the larger, fatter man as if he were merely regarding an insignificant little bug that he was about to squash under his shoe without even blinking an eye.

The larger man faltered and raised his gun back up towards the Beast, the muzzle obviously shaking which would practically render the weapon useless to anyone who was trying to fire it. The squid-like creature leapt off the man with its tentacles extended but the Beast's jaws made quick work of snapping the thing into three separate pieces without even pausing.

"You?"

The Beast tilted his head to the side. "Yes, me."

Grabbing hold of the arm that held the gun, the Beast pulled Father Glaz towards him before slamming a fist straight into his gut to dig his claws in as deep as he possibly could. The weapon clattered uselessly towards the ground, the metallic sound ringing in the strange room and for a moment Charlie wondered where she had put the gun she had picked up before. She did not get the chance to think long about it as Father Glaz was thrown towards the opposite side of the room with a bone-breaking crunch.

Father Glaz somehow managed to pick himself up from the fall, however, and pointed a very shaky finger towards the Beast. "I will send you back to Hell, to atone for all your sins."

A snort was sent his way. "My sins? You know nothing of them." A deep growl came from inside the man's chest. "But since you seem so keen to see what Hell is really like, let me ensure that your little pathetic black soul arrives there on a silver platter to be devoured by the things worse than me!"

The Beast launched himself forward with a snarl that shook the foundations around them. In a rush of black fur he brought back the vigour of the creature who had previously taken a swipe at the shark-faced man. With an explosion of movement, the Beast slashed straight through Father Glaz's bulging stomach.

Closing her eyes, Charlie threw herself back behind the piece of furniture that she had hidden behind and covered her ears for good measure. Whilst she had lived with the terrible Lights and the things that they had done over the long time that she had been with them, it never meant that she willingly took to watching the terrifying acts that some could do to others. If only to spare herself from a lifetime of nightmares. Vaguely she recalled the times when, in a deranged panic, she had thought of being the one who was delivering the pain and punishment. She had frightened herself too much; there was no way she would be willing to do those things herself.

She would rather be forced to live in the dark and never see the light of day again than deliver a blow to someone else. Except in extreme circumstances where her survival depended on it.

Inhale.

Exhale.

Inhale.

Exhale.

It'll be alright soon.

After a time, Charlie's arms started to feel numb and slowly she lowered them, fully prepared to throw them back up should she start hearing the sounds that she did not want to hear. But there was only silence, causing her to open one eye and then another.

Still silence and nothing else.

Very slowly, Charlie leaned around to peek at where the Beast and Father Glaz had been. She found herself surprisingly calm when all she saw was the strange human-like figure wearing the Beast's head. He was kneeling on the ground, not quite in prayer but clearly thinking something deep and metaphorical. It made her take light footsteps as she approached him. The stench of blood was in the air, as well as other bodily fluids, but also tinged with fear and anger the likes of which the Lights never really left behind.

Taking careful steps forward, Charlie was able to focus on the space beyond the Beast, though she was having difficulty focusing her gaze. Father Glaz no longer had a body, not anymore. The only reason she even really realised there was anything left of him was that half a head was lying on the ground, the skin flopping down in sick folds that really made it appear that the man had stolen the skin of someone else. Charlie wouldn't put it past the man as he had always been extremely unsettling to look at.

The red stains on the wall were almost an improvement to the dull slabs of wood that had been there before, were it not for the macabre feeling it gave the room. How anyone could have ever felt relaxed in a place like this was beyond Charlie's understanding.

She stepped closer to the Beast, tentatively reaching out a hand to touch his shoulder. It caused an automatic tensioning, but a single glance brought him back to the present moment. He looked at his hands for a second or two, dropping something wet and squelchy to the ground before raising his head.

"Do you remember your parents?" he asked, his voice soft and understanding.

Charlie thought about it for a few seconds. "I....do not.... know."

"Do you remember anything before the Lights?" came an even softer voice, that spoke to Charlie's instincts so clearly. It was as if she needed to be reminded that this unfamiliar man was safe, would look after her and make sure that she was safe regardless of the consequences.

For a few long moments, Charlie considered the Beast's question. Her head tilted up towards the ceiling and she blinked. "I remember the sun. How it was always warm and welcoming. The trees in the local park. Bob the church cat who was the only one that I was really friends with...I know there was someone...but they never came for me."

The realisation struck Charlie hard, causing an unexpected sob to escape from her lips. "They just...they left me. They let Father Glaz take me away...they didn't even fight him."

Those big, strong arms that she had felt before, wrapped tightly around her frame, surrounding her with warmth, love, and a willingness to protect. The Beast let out a sound that could be best described as a purr whilst Charlie continued to sob, wail and screech because there was nothing left for her to do. She wasn't chastised for her crying. She wasn't told to shut up and take it like the little bitch that she was. Instead, she was just wrapped up in a feeling of security, the love she should have always been given and the confidence that nothing like this would ever happen to her again.

Vaguely she became aware that at some point she had been lifted into the Beast's arms, carried along seemingly endless corridors with virtually all their doors thrown open in some way and a new scent reached her.

Fresh air.

Rain.

Steaming hot tea.

Something sweet.

Inviting.

Safe.

Opening her pale eyes as drops of water landed on her cheeks, Charlie looked up into a grey sky and blinked repeatedly. Even though the sunlight was dimmed through the rain, she still had to shield her eyes from it with a pained sound before her brain registered that this was the outside. Her head turned this way and that. She took in the road, the cars, and the other tall buildings that surrounded the building they had just left as they emerged into a throng of people.

Not Lights, not Father Glaz, no priests, or overseers. Only those who had been so far away from everything that nobody had been allowed to talk about them in front of the young ones. The men and women who would come around often to try and gain entry or ask questions that were never answered. They only ever caused more shouting and arguing. It took Charlie a few moments to recall the word 'police', but she had no real idea of what they were or if they could help her.

The Beast, however, made his way confidently through the crowd of police, some of whom were restraining Lights and asking questions. Some others were studying various documents and papers to see if they held any types of information on the Lights. Others busied themselves sorting out the syringes that contained the glowing green liquids that gave Charlie headaches and strange visions. The girl turned away from that, burying her head into the chest of the man carrying her and letting his aura of safety wash over her. She was fine as long as she was with the Beast so nothing bad could happen to her here.

None of the police seemed to notice them as they walked past, too absorbed in what they were doing while the Lights recoiled away in panic and fright, some screaming incoherently, others whimpering and cowering where they stood. One raised his head, half his face clawed off and screamed, "There's the fucker! With the abomination! I'll cut his throat out!"

The man barely made it two steps towards them before the other half of his face was clawed with freshly splattered blood covering the startled police officer. The Beast continued forward, ignoring the commotion he had just caused. Charlie was confused for a few seconds, but decided not to question anything as there were already too many questions in her mind to really focus on any one thing. She leaned her head back and just allowed herself to drift in the safety she felt.

Eventually the Beast came to a stop in front of a man who seemed important as he was dressed a little differently from the police, but he wasn't a Light or one of the priests. He wore a light tan suit, his brown hair gelled back from his face and thick-rimmed, square glasses covering his eyes that were heterochromatic, the right one being a bright blue whilst the left was a deep emerald green. Each one glistened with some strange platinum marks that seemed to change patterns every time he blinked. Until they focused directly on Charlie and the Beast, where they became a permanently lidded eye with a loop underneath it. The term 'Eye of Horace' floated up from the back of Charlie's mind, but she had no real reason for knowing it.

The man jolted a little, as if surprised before letting out a breath through his nose. "I should have known it would be you."

The Beast gave no response, staying silent for the time being.

"I take it, this is one of those cases?" the man continued, seeming to be unbothered by the lack of response, almost as if he had dealt with the Beast before.

Charlie was confused by that as she was pretty much convinced that any adult who dealt with the Beast would end up dead before long, but she kept her mouth shut. "Will this explain where Father Glaz is right now, Beast?"

"Spooner," came the straight reply, before Charlie was offered towards the man. "Take her away. Make her safe. Make her happy."

Spooner accepted Charlie who immediately felt distressed at the notion of the Beast leaving her, but the creature leaned closer to gently nuzzle his face into hers with a huff. "He's a good man, he'll make sure you live the life you deserve."

Tears stung at Charlie's eyes as the red and black fur pulled away, the man replaced with the four pawed version that seemed to regard the pair before nodding and turning away. Spooner however had another question brimming on his lips. "Where's the other one?"

Charlie blinked, feeling a stab of fear through her heart that there was possibly someone else in this mess of a world who had gone through the same sort of treatment as herself. A large, very soft hand landed on her face though to caress it and settle her down with a gentle sigh. "She normally comes snooping around after you. It's like she's drawn to you."

"She does not follow me," came the straightforward reply.

"Oh, she does," Spooner replied, "Whether it be conscious or not. So where is she?"

The Beast shook his large head and started padding off the way he had come, refusing to answer any more questions. He summoned up a portal in a nearby wall that pulsated a mixture of purples and blacks. For a second, he seemed to pause, lifting his head up into the air to sniff a couple of times, before the red eyes refocused and with a bound the Beast charged straight through the portal and out into wherever it was that his next meal was coming from.

Spooner blew out a sigh, dropping his gaze down to Charlie who noticed that the Eye of Horace disappeared to turn into a series of different shapes again every time he blinked. "What's your name, little one?"

"Charlie," the girl replied, feeling a little nervous before glancing back towards the wall. "Will he come back?"

"I do not know," Spooner replied. "He'll be off to help someone else though. That much I know."

"He is a good dog," Charlie replied, feeling suddenly very tired.

"Hmm," Spooner replied, turning his head away from Charlie to scan the crowd and just for a moment seeing a black-cloaked figure with a white mask standing with the most longing look in the soft, grey, cat-like eyes. The slightest turn of the head was enough to let Spooner know that she had caught him, as the next blink the figure was gone from view. Spooner sighed, shaking his head.

Charlie did not pay attention as finally she felt free to just fall into a restful sleep in the arms of this strange, wonderful man who would surely help her.

The lights could no longer reach her.

Father Glaz was a bloodied wreck down below them.

She was free.

BAD RABBIT

A shiver ran through Patsy at the sight of the box. It looked simple enough, a little on the large side but otherwise plain and nondescript. The only thing that made it remarkable was a small white triangle on the top-right corner.

It was back to haunt her, always keeping its vile and twisted promise.

She looked to the figure standing next to her, eyes wide and innocent as they took in the smooth, white mask of a cat, the details painted with a stunning silver that reflected the light. "It's back," she stuttered out, shivering again.

A single beat carried through the darkness that surrounded them on this long, twisted driveway that the pair had been walking down. The grey stones constantly crunched under her trainers, whilst the trees were gnarled, twisted ancient beings that leaned dangerously over to snag at Patsy's dyed, golden hair. The air was stale, like an unused basement where one was forbidden to go because of the bad rabbit that resided there. The one that would gobble up pretty, innocent, angelic children like Patsy and spit out their bones on the doorstep to be found later by terrified parents frantic with worry. Patsy's father had bolted the basement door firmly, telling her to never open it no matter what she heard.

Only for the doorbell to ring in the next morning, with a large box appearing on the doorstep with a white triangle on it. Patsy knew what was held inside each time and watched with growing terror as her father would remove the lid, lift out the contents and then turn towards her with the most terrified expression on his face.

In his hands would be a large, ragged, stuffed rabbit. Old, battered and stitched together so many times over that the original colour of the fur was now a graphite-grey with patches that seemed too dark to have been placed deliberately. Patsy had tried to run away in the beginning, tried so many ways to get rid of the rabbit with the haunted, clear, glass eyes but it was to no avail. Bad Rabbit always returned to her, seeking her out with a sole mission to torment her to the end of her days.

The figure in the black cloak with the white cat-mask merely regarded Patsy. At first, upon finding the silent walker, Patsy had presumed they were a nun or a follower of some religion that required them to be covered in a long, black cloak that almost appeared to be made from the shadows itself. The cat-mask was a stark contrast, a beautiful porcelain-white with just the merest hints of silver outlines to give definition to the creature that was supposed to be represented. However, behind the eye-slits were not human eyes, in fact there were no eyes at all. Just a slowly twirling mass of rust-red that sometimes sparkled when another colour would briefly appear. Patsy did not know if she should fear this stranger, who only called herself The Collector, with a soft, feminine voice that was a mere whisper on the wind. However she did know what true fear was and it was hidden in the box with the white triangle only a few feet away from her.

The rust coloured eye-slits turned black for a second, as if the other was blinking before returning to what they had been before. "What are you going to do about it?" came the whisper as a reply.

Patsy blinked and took half a step back in shock. "Me?"

The Collector turned to look at the box which was standing exactly where they had left it. "Yes. It is merely a mortal object which I do not deal with."

Patsy frowned at the stranger before whimpering as she turned back to the box, "But Bad Rabbit is in there and Bad Rabbit does bad things to people."

"Does it now?" the Collector commented, tilting her head slightly to the side.

A sound came from the box, a mixture of gurgles and snorts that sounded like something choking on water and Patsy turned away. Her eyes scoured the ground, looking for anything that could protect her from Bad Rabbit and her eyes fell onto a long piece of pipe. Grabbing the metal, an ice-cold pain shot straight up her arms she turned back to the box with narrowed eyes. "I won't let Bad Rabbit do anything bad to me. Bad Rabbit took everything from me."

She stepped forward, the gurgling sounds more intense now, and raised the metal pipe above her head. "You hear me Bad Rabbit? This is how you end! By my hands after you took everything from me!"

With one fell swoop the pipe passed into the box, crushing the cardboard and causing a high pitched scream of pain from inside. Patsy swung the pipe repeatedly, hitting the box time and time again, the choked squealing inside getting higher and more frantic before finally stopping with a terrible sounding squelch. Patsy stepped back as something oozed out of the gaps in the cardboard and dropped the pipe to the ground. She let out a long breath and raised her eyes towards the onyx-black sky where only the sliver of the moon was visible.

"Do you think it's over?" the Collector's voice whispered on the wind.

Patsy looked down at her feet, surprised to see the box was gone from where it had been and allowed a large smile to cross her face. "Yes," she called brightly, taking hold of the skeletal hand in pure glee then began skipping on down the path with its twisted trees and crunchy gravel. A laugh on her lips and the sense of freedom in her chest.

Until they rounded a corner and standing in the centre of the road was a large, nondescript box with a white triangle in the corner. This time there were long, spider web threads of temptress-red creeping down from the top, just under the lid.

Patsy stopped dead and stared in terror, snapping her head back behind her to see if the other box was there. It was gone, not a single trace remaining, and she shuddered violently. "How does Bad Rabbit do that?! Every single time I get rid of it, it comes back."

"Do you really get rid of it?" asked the Collector. "Or do you just pretend?"

A snarl left Patsy's lips as she turned back to the figure, ripping her hand out of the one she had opted to hold just a few moments before. "Of course it comes back, you've literally just seen it happen. Father always locked it away, made sure that it was secured in the basement and still Bad Rabbit always came back."

She stormed angrily towards the box, her memories flashing of the times that she had watched the man barely escape with his life. Scratch marks all down his arms, bite marks on his face and bruises forming from the beatings that Bad Rabbit had delivered. The way he'd slam the door to the basement shut, slam the bolt into place and yell at his wife to bring the extra strong padlocks. Bad Rabbit would screech and scream for the next hour, shouting horrendous curses and vile words out of its mouth all the while smacking the interior door until exhaustion or boredom would force it to stop.

Patsy remembered sitting in the living room, remaining still and quiet whilst her mother would use the first aid kit on her father. Speaking in whispers that she was not meant to overhear but did anyway because she was always the good, quiet girl who remained just out of sight. The one who followed the rules, who never spilled anything and who never went near the basement door. The sweet, angelic, little girl who would follow her parents up to bed after each and every outburst from Bad Rabbit. She would go to her room and kneel to pray to the Holy God to free them of this cursed beast before laying down in bed and sleeping with the night light on. Bad Rabbit did not like the light, would never come into her room if it was bright.

Unlike Patsy, her parents preferred to remain in the darkness, keeping their distance from the monster that they held in the basement. They tried to stay away from those other strange adults who would appear sometimes, sounding concerned and wanting to help but none of them ever did. Patsy would watch them, silent, angelic and perfect in every single way. When they asked her about

Bad Rabbit she would never comment. Although one time when they pressed, she said that it was her pet bunny rabbit that had gotten too big and had to be kept in the basement to be fed on the neighbours' carrots. The adults who were talking to her wanted to see Bad Rabbit, to confirm that it was indeed what she claimed and since her parents were talking to other adults in a different room, she agreed.

Their screams were short-lived, their bodies were heavy and when her parents stood at the edge of the hole they had dug, Patsy witnessed Bad Rabbit charging at them with blood red eyes and nothing short of murderous intentions. Neither one of her parents screamed, but she supposed that screaming was not an option when a knife was stabbed directly through the back of your throat. Bad Rabbit threw the bodies into the open grave and then made Patsy cover them up, saying that if she did so then Bad Rabbit would become her best friend and protect her forever. Patsy did not believe Bad Rabbit but had known it was likely her only chance to survive.

Her attention returned to the present as she glared at the box again, that was still and silent this time and found herself seething. "Bad Rabbit was always the liar, said one thing and then would deliberately do another. Always broke promises and never shared any of its secrets with me."

As Patsy spoke, she looked around for something to help her deal with the situation. A sparkle caught her eye and she was surprised to see the moonlight glimmering off a kitchen knife that was embedded in a gnarled and twisted tree trunk nearby. But she turned her head away and instead spotted a large pile of rocks. "Help me move these," she instructed the Collector who was still standing in the same spot that she had been before.

"For what purpose?" came the whispered question, as if a wind was blowing through the corners of a creaky old house.

Patsy had picked up a large rock, heavier than she could normally lift but adrenaline was rushing through her system which she supposed provided her with a little extra strength. She could barely stagger under the weight as she moved to the box and then lifted it up high above her head. "A dead body is harder to move when it's weighed down."

The rock dropped easily from her hands, crushing through the cardboard and connecting with something that was clearly organic from the dull thud it made. "Bad Rabbit taught me that," she continued, grabbing another rock and dropping it with a heavy clunk next to the one that she had already dropped. "Made me do it to those girls in the woods."

"Which girls?" the Collector asked, having not moved from her spot.

"Those beautiful, talented girls from our local ballet school," Patsy continued, dropping another rock in with a hollow sound. "The angels who were the apples of everyone's eyes. So sweet, so charming, so irresistible."

Another rock thumped into place. "Everyone loved them. Everyone cared for them. They made cookies and sold them to make money for the poor kids. They got everyone in class to club together to buy me a Christmas present because they knew I had no mother or father of my own."

Clack, thud.

"They went to the woods one day with Bad Rabbit," Patsy continued, adding yet another rock to the pile that she had already created. "I don't know why? I warned them about Bad Rabbit. That they were not to go with Bad Rabbit should it tempt them any-where. But they went."

Another rock landed.

"I found them, once Bad Rabbit was done." Patsy sighed as she bent to pick up another rock and moved it towards the growing pile. "They drank some tea Bad Rabbit gave them, and it made them sleep. Bad Rabbit then found rocks and dropped them on top of their pretty little heads. It took me hours to cover them."

Clack, thud.

"So many hours," Patsy continued, picking up the final rock and placing it on top.

"The night had long set in when I had finished and my hands were scuffed and bruised. Bad Rabbit just patted me on the head and gave me a library card. It said that if anyone asked, I had been in the library all night and not to tell the adults in blue where the bodies were."

Patsy stepped back, looking at the rocks. "I never got asked. I just stayed at the place where I was living and faked being ill for a month until I could face going back. There were no more smiles in that school, and no one played games anymore."

Shaking her head, Patsy glared at the rock pile. "You better stay there, Bad Rabbit. Because next time I won't be so nice to you."

She started away, down the long driveway that she had no ac-tual memory of starting to walk down or reason as to why. She had been at home, taking time to read and have a well deserved cup of tea before someone rang her doorbell. When she answered, there was a package sitting on her doorstep, plain and unaddressed with a single white triangle on the right corner. Patsy yelled and kicked the box back down the stairs. She then took off in a run in the op-posite direction which led her to a long driveway that she couldn't even see the end of. It did occur to her that this was strange, because she lived in the inner city, well away from rural areas and there were no forests nearby.

Pausing, she turned to look back at the Collector who was following behind her with measured, silent steps. "Where are we?"

"A place between," was the near silent answer.

"Between what?" Patsy snapped.

"I do not know," the Collector replied, though turned her head away from Patsy. "I merely seek those who are here, but I've never actually questioned where."

A frown crossed the pretty, angelic expression that Patsy wore. "You speak like Bad Rabbit."

"Do I?" the Collector asked. "Or is that how you choose to hear it speak?"

"What does that even mean?" Patsy snapped back towards the Collector, suddenly disliking her presence. No longer was she a comfort, a wandering soul who happened to be in the right place. Now the presumed woman was a potential threat. Someone that would ask too many questions. If there was one thing that the Patsy did not like, it was questions.

Everyone always had questions for her. Questions about the past, questions about those she knew and questions about Bad Rabbit. It was the threat that she warned them all constantly about but nobody ever took her seriously.

"Do you actually hear Bad Rabbit speak or are you just pretending to?" the Collector asked again.

Patsy snarled. "I don't pretend. I've never pretended in my life, yet everyone treats me as if I do every damn day. No one has ever believed me about Bad Rabbit! How it keeps turning up and taking everything from me. You're no different from any other, just like Bad Rabbit said you'd be."

Another slow, deliberate dark blink passed over the rust-red eyes behind the white cat-mask, turning the eyeholes completely black for a few seconds before the colour returned with slivers of white that slowly spiralled to make a tiny, white pupil in the centre. "How could Bad Rabbit know me, if it's not here in the in-between?"

"Not here!" Patsy shrieked and pointed towards the pile of rocks. "Bad Rabbit is buried right there under all my hard work! Which you did absolutely nothing to help with by the way!"

Another moment of silence before the Collector responded. "Which pile are you talking about?"

Snapping her head to the side, all the fury she had felt before melted into terror upon finding herself staring down a long empty driveway with gnarled, twisted, black trees creating a canopy. The heavy, grey gravel crunched under her trainers and a hollow sounding wind whistled past her. There was no mound of rocks, no indication that she had been walking for miles and as she turned back to look at the Collector, there again was the same, nondescript box in the road. It looked just like it had before except now it had additional red lines running down the sides whilst the lid had crease marks on it as if it had been pushed back out after being crushed under something heavy.

Patsy staggered backwards; her face contorted in fear. She shakily raised her finger up towards the strangely attired woman. "You're in league with Bad Rabbit, aren't you? You've tricked me to this place and it's just torturing me because I would no longer do its bad biddings."

The Collector observed the girl quietly for a few seconds. "You uphold Bad Rabbit even when presented with the truth?"

Standing upright, Patsy snarled once again and picked up a smaller rock which happened to be by her foot and launched it at the cat-mask wearing figure. "What have you shown me? You're just like everyone else, bewitched by Bad Rabbit to turn against me so that I can have nothing of my own!"

She picked up a much larger rock and flung it at the Collector, her rage boiling over harshly, "Everyone always asks questions. They say that I'm lying about Bad Rabbit and say that I'm crazy when I'm not. You're just like that patronising psychologist, saying that I repressed everything behind an illusion! Bad Rabbit was standing right there telling her everything about me and what to think!" Another rock ended up in her hands and Patsy stormed towards the still standing figure. "You know what he did to that idiot woman eventually?"

"No," the Collector replied in that same monotone voice that had been used throughout their whole exchange.

Patsy did not answer.

There was only a singular crack as the cat-mask fell clean away in two separate pieces towards the ground whilst the black cloak shimmered down into a pool of inky blackness that remained still. Patsy blinked, staring in confusion towards the two pieces and lowered herself down to the ground to lightly poke at the porcelain. "See, Bad Rabbit got you, just like all the others who doubted me."

She stood up and let the rock fall back into the inky mess. "Now, how do I..."

There came a rustling noise from behind her and Patsy turned towards the dented and stained box with the white triangle. She had nearly forgotten about it whilst she was dealing with the mysterious figure who had asked so many questions. The box was moving of its own accord, shaking slightly as if something inside was growing. The lid clattered to the ground as a low, harrowing moan began to sound.

Patsy let out a gasp.

Rising out of the box was Bad Rabbit. Around five feet tall, with manky grey fur, patchwork hastily sewn in place with uneven stitches, a popped out bead for an eye which clung to a piece of thread and the overall look of something which had been abandoned a long time ago. The one remaining eye shone with a brilliant, blinding-white that moved back and forth like it could not decide where to look. Patsy got the distinct impression that Bad Rabbit was looking for someone and was having trouble adjusting to this new, larger form.

Bad Rabbit's head snapped to look directly at Patsy, the large ears flopping to the right as its head tilted in the same direction. A sound cut through the harrowing moan, a note of joy and happiness as if Bad Rabbit had recognised her as someone so important and special.

It raised its arms out towards her, a twisted smile forming on the lips as a call of, "Am Am!" came across them.

Patsy stepped back. "Stay away!"

"Am Am!" came the more joyous shout from Bad Rabbit once again as it staggered towards her.

"No!" Patsy shrieked, backing away from the creature of her nightmares. "You stay away from me you little freak."

"Am Am!" The voice now took on a longer formation for each word, almost as if it were singing. It sounded so happy to see her.

As if this messed up creature's entire world only revolved around Patsy and absolutely nothing else mattered.

Looking down to grab yet another rock, Patsy found that the gravel pathway which had previously been under her feet had given way to a beautifully soft, dark green carpet with the vague outlines of happy little creatures on it but smeared with dirt and grime. She looked up and found that no longer was she on the long, winding path with the gnarled trees. Now there were walls around her that may have once been a pretty blue colour but were heavily stained a sickening green whilst huge, indescribable shadows stuck out at odd angles. It almost reminded Patsy of a nursery. One that hopefully hadn't housed children for quite some time. A putrid stench filled the air, making Patsy want to gag as it invaded her nose and mouth, but she still turned and ran.

It was the only thing that she could do to survive at this point.

Clearly Bad Rabbit had dragged her into some place where she would be vulnerable enough to be trapped so that it could do whatever it wanted to her, and Patsy was not going to allow that to happen. She had escaped every single attempt on her life before and had warned so many people that bad things would come to them if they got too close, but it had all been in vain.

She vowed that she would not become one of its victims.

"Am Am!" came the cry from Bad Rabbit, sounding distraught and almost screeching the words now as it continued to stagger after her.

Patsy shook her head as she ran. "Fuck off you little piece of shit! I am not going to fall for that."

She turned a corner, passed several shadowed objects lying in her path and found the stench getting worse. She choked on the air, desperate to get rid of the smell but finding it to no avail. Still she pushed on, trying not to focus on the constant shuffling that signalled Bad Rabbit was close by. Never quite enough to reach her but always just at the edge of her vision no matter which way she turned.

Until she came up against a wall. One where the putrid stench turned into a vaporous cloud that was thick in the air and could be best described as a collection of filthy clothes, unwashed plates, mouldy take-out boxes and various bottles of half-finished formula that was covered in mounds of ash. Patsy coughed harshly and stepped away from the wall, eyes streaming with the uttermost disgust and found herself crashing into Bad Rabbit.

"Am Am!" it cried happily again, trying to wrap its arms around her in a hug.

Patsy screamed the loudest she had ever done in her life and pushed Bad Rabbit away. It stumbled back, making a confused sound as if it could not comprehend what was going on and Patsy took her opportunity. A glass bottle was ripped out of the nearest pile of rubbish and smashed against a post to break it cleanly in two.

She then drove it straight into the face of Bad Rabbit with a snarl. "Your pathetic little game is over! Stop haunting me and leave me alone!"

Thrusting the bottle forward, Patsy watched as Bad Rabbit staggered backwards once again. Suddenly its head snapped back so sharply that Patsy was sure she had heard its neck breaking. The body remained upright and the head was tilted backwards at a near impossible angle and for a few long seconds, silence reigned.

Patsy let out a sigh of relief, dropping the bottle to the ground as the world faded away and she felt truly free for the first time in a long while.

Crunch.

Bad Rabbit's head snapped back into place, the once glowing, white eye now seeping with blood that turned from a milky pink to darkest red. A hollow laugh, one that came from the very depths of Hell itself echoed all around the strange new space, before a deep voice with a sinister edge taunted Patsy. "Naughty Am Am, you shouldn't have done that."

"How are you even-" Patsy started.

"Because you want me to be," Bad Rabbit replied, lifting a heavy pole in its left hand, "Because you need me to be."

Patsy shook her head, "I never wanted you! You destroy everything that I love, and no one believes me."

"Are you sure about that, Am Am?" Bad Rabbit replied, the heavy pole in its hand flicking to land in the other hand with a smack that revealed a large axe head attached. "Or is this just make-believe?"

A scream escaped Patsy's lips as Bad Rabbit raised the axe up above its head and brought it down mere inches from her body. "Shall we play a little game? Like the one we played with those little ones in the back streets? Shall I be it?"

All the colour drained from Patsy's face, remembering that incident well. Bad Rabbit convinced all the local children to play hide and go seek with a twist. When the person who was it found someone, they were to place a large red sticker on their body and pretend to cut them down with an axe that had been found in one of the parent's back yards. Patsy had been the last to be found, when Bad Rabbit's axe was covered in red, but the way it dripped certainly did not resemble stickers.

"No!" she whispered. "Leave me alone! I never did anything wrong. It was always you."

"I'll start at ten," Bad Rabbit said, hauling the axe back out of the ground. "You must hide Am Am, so I can come and find you."

Staring at the insane creature which had haunted her for years, Patsy tried to believe that none of this was real. That she was just in the middle of a very bad nightmare that was going to have her shooting up in bed at any moment. She would search the house, realise that it was just a bad dream and then laugh at herself before getting ready for the date that she had planned.

"Ten," boomed Bad Rabbit, its voice still echoing and large.

Patsy closed her eyes tightly, willing all this terror and madness to go away.

"Nine," continued Bad Rabbit.

It was all a dream, a nightmare, none of it was real. She was just lying in her bed, all comfy and soft and had eaten some cheese or that curry from the place down the way that had something in it that was giving her trippy dreams.

"Eight."

She couldn't be in this situation, it was impossible for a large, soft rabbit toy to be chasing her with an axe. The idea was just stupid and silly.

"Seven."

Well behaved little girls always told the truth and never did anything wrong. Patsy was a good little girl. She had just attracted the attention of a demon who liked nothing more than to take away everything that she had ever loved.

"Six."

This was a dream. It was all make-believe and make-believe did not exist. It was where the bad things were. Where the naughty monsters who did nasty things to people were. She should never believe in make-believe because it was not real. Bad Rabbit was not real, not in the sense that anyone ever understood of course, but that was their fault. She had never done anything wrong.

"Five." A chuckle escaped from Bad Rabbit. "I'm going to slice you up if you don't run, Am Am."

Patsy ignored the voice; it was all a trick. All fake words being spoken by a fake person who never existed. Like that time when that dreary social worker came knocking on the door to ask about some baby that had gone missing from the neighbour's garden. The neighbours had said they saw her going into the garden to play with the baby, but Patsy never had. She did not like children, they were noisy, got in the way of adult life and she would never allow one to interrupt her day.

Especially when the parents couldn't be bothered to look after the whiny little mite. Bad Rabbit had been lurking in the corner of the garden, eyeing up the prize so Patsy had gone to check on the child, was satisfied that it was fine and then left. If anyone had taken it, then it must be Bad Rabbit because that was what Bad Rabbit did.

"Four."

Patsy had heard eventually that the baby had been found in the woods some distance away, though it wasn't alive. Because of course it wouldn't be alive. Bad Rabbit killed anything soft, innocent and pure.

"Three"

She could still see the horrified looks in her adoptive parents' eyes, as they lay on the kitchen floor, choking on their blood from the knife wounds across their necks. Patsy had looked down at their gasping bodies, aware that Bad Rabbit was standing just behind her, and whispered, "I told you Bad Rabbit would come get you, but you didn't listen."

"Two."

Patsy resolved herself to not moving another step because this was all make-believe. It was completely fake and nothing that she had to worry about because it was not real. Bad Rabbit was trying to punish her for not providing it any more victims as she preferred to live a solitary life away from people. Away from snooping, pesky people who stuck their noses in where they weren't wanted. Where there were no idiotic doctors, raving mad psychologists or social workers who were trying their best to help but were all just as illusionary as Bad Rabbit.

Patsy did not play make-believe, she spoke only the truth, and no one would ever believe her until it was too late.

"One."

Silence reigned afterwards. The stench disappeared and the odd coldness that she had been feeling only moments ago also went away. It was strange how the senses worked, how they noticed things only in their absence or at their departure, despite having been around the whole time. A single clock started ticking in the background, her clock. The one she had claimed from a skip outside a house that was being cleared. Bad Rabbit had disappeared inside the house to grab a multitude of other things and then hidden them in Patsy's home, but Patsy knew better than to keep the stolen items on display. She couldn't even return them to their owners. How would that look? She had hidden them in a place where no one would look or ask pesky questions.

She took a deep breath, and she recognised the scent of honeydew and lavender. It was from the infuser that she used and knew that she was home. Safe, sound and perfectly free of all the madness.

She opened her eyes.

The axe head missed her by mere millimetres as it swung down into her floor. Patsy screamed and staggered backwards, finding Bad Rabbit directly in front of her with a distorted smile on its face that looked almost human.

"Game on," was all it said as it ripped the axe back out of the floor.

Patsy turned and ran as fast as she could as the laughter of Bad Rabbit echoed back from all the familiar nooks and crannies of her house. She knew that she couldn't stop or else she would be caught and killed by Bad Rabbit, and she still had so much to do with her life. A dresser crashed to the ground as she pulled it down behind her, trying to halt the progress of the axe-wielding maniac behind her whilst she desperately tried to think of how she was going to get out of this situation. Bad Rabbit would stop at nothing to get her, she knew that, and everything would be over if he caught up with her.

A sudden thought flashed into her mind, and it renewed all her hope.

She had a gun, a big gun, which was down in her basement. She used it to keep people away from her property and occasionally go hunting for game. The door to the basement could be easily locked and bolted from the other side and Bad Rabbit would take an age to get through it. Pausing momentarily, she heard the dresser that she had pulled down behind her disintegrate into more pieces as Bad Rabbit stormed straight through it. Patsy got her bearings and realised that she was on the top floor, in an unfurnished room which she had just never gotten around to decorating.

Patsy rushed through the opposite door as she heard Bad Rabbit call out, "Found you, Am Am!" She heard a crunch as it smacked its axe into the floor where she had previously been standing. Desperately she grabbed the banister and vaulted down the stairs taking three at a time. Several pot plants crashed into the floor as she dodged around the debris, far too used to ducking and diving out of the way of much more dangerously thrown objects.

Dangerously thrown objects like knives, which the cook at her last job had started throwing at her during one service because she had misplaced two orders, and he was getting frustrated at having to cook all the food again. A slight graze had been Patsy's reward for all her hard work and once the manager had calmed everything down, no action was taken against either one of them. Most of the waiting staff had sided with the chef, saying that Patsy always messed up orders deliberately and caused issues every time she was in, but Patsy had protested her innocence, stating that it must be Bad Rabbit causing issues for her.

They had all called her crazy and a variety of other nasty names as well. Patsy had warned them that if they continued then Bad Rabbit would more than likely come and get them because she loved her job, and they all just sneered at her. Then a few weeks later, Patsy called sick and then heard on the news of the devastating tale that all the workers in the restaurant had been poisoned with botulinum, which had caused their nervous systems to fail. It had to have been a painful death. Several customers had witnessed it and the only possible source was someone putting a large amount in the water tank that fed the staff rooms at the back of the building.

Patsy had been the only one to notice Bad Rabbit dancing in the background to only a song that it could possibly hear, and she had quickly turned off the TV with a severe feeling of sickness in her stomach.

The axe lodged into the floor with a loud thwack just behind her as she dodged around a corner. It brought her back to the present and spurred her on.

She moved through the kitchen and to the basement door. Then another thought flashed into her mind, causing her to spin back around. There was a huge water tank by the side of the boxes. She had installed it to try and prove to the water board that she was not using as much water as they had claimed. It turned out that Bad Rabbit liked to flood her kitchen and bathroom every single week. Exactly why was beyond her but right now the tank would be a perfect solution. She rushed across, grabbed the edge and hauled it straight over.

A scream left her lips when, along with the torrent of water, the small bodies of several kittens and puppies cascaded onto her floor. It was all she could do to ignore them for now. She didn't have the time, nor the patience left to deal with anything like this. Scrabbling upright as she heard the familiar thumping of Bad Rabbit's large feet, Patsy charged straight to the door to the basement and propped it open before leaping down two of the steps.

"Am Am, you're being a very silly girl." Bad Rabbit's voice echoed hollowly back as the huge figure appeared in the doorway to the kitchen. "You know I can find you anywhere you go."

"Not this time, freak!" Patsy jeered. "I'm done with you Bad Rabbit, I'm done with you destroying everything good in my life, taking away anything that might be good. You never give me a break! I could have been so happy, so free and so loved if not for your constant interference."

Bad Rabbit snorted, taking half a step into the kitchen. "You still live in your make-believe world, don't you Patsy?"

"Make-believe does not exist," Patsy hissed. "It never has existed. You just warp everyone's perception so that they don't see you, don't hear you and then blame everything on me. I'm a good girl, I did everything right, followed all the instructions and was so nice to everyone. Despite that you caused me nothing but pain, grief, and terror for all these years."

Again, there was a shake of the head, this time Bad Rabbit strode into the kitchen with very deliberate steps that allowed the water to soak up into his feet. "Do you really believe that Patsy? That you're a good girl? That you are being terrorised by a demon who wants nothing more than to see you suffer for eternity?"

"You're telling me this when you are clearly that demon!" Patsy snarled back, feeling her arms beginning to shake.

Bad Rabbit chuckled. "Did you ever think that just maybe, this was all your doing?"

Patsy blinked, lowering her shoulders just a little bit as confusion crossed her face. "What?"

"All this death, all this destruction, all the times that something went wrong or something was taken from you," Bad Rabbit continued. "Could it be that it was you all along?"

The thought was completely absurd in Patsy's opinion. She had never done a bad thing in her life. She had tried to warn everyone and had told them of the dangers of befriending her. She had warned them that there was something very evil that lurked around the corners of the world and that it would strike if they got too close. Most simply called her names or said that she was crazy. They got her tested for various ailments and tried to speak to her in that patronising tone as if she were some insane, dangerous animal that was going to snap at any moment and kill them all.

Sometimes she wished that they would drop dead just so they would stop bothering her. None of them would open their eyes and see what was right in front of them as clear as day.

The looming figure of Bad Rabbit, who was grinning manically at her from every reflective surface, was always just visible in the corner of her eye. Always present to remind her that it would be there to take things away, that it would destroy whatever beautiful moment of peace she had found. So, she tried to never get attached or to distance herself, but it never worked.

But for this monster to suggest that this was all her doing, that somehow, she was the one causing all of this.

She scowled. "That's what you want to trick me with, isn't it? Just to make sure that you can go on doing all your bad things because you have no other way to live. I have never done a bad thing in my life; it's always only been you. Ever since that day you turned up in that box, you've been nothing but a constant thorn in my side…"

She took note of the fact that Bad Rabbit was now standing in the centre of the kitchen, water soaking all the way up its legs. Except for the wooden step that she was standing on. "But no longer! I'll deal with you once and for all and send you back to Hell where you belong! You deserve to stay there for all eternity!"

She leapt up onto the countertop with ease. She had always been extremely flexible and filled with a natural bounce. It should have allowed her on any gymnastics or cheerleading team but she was never picked. Never pretty enough, never good enough and always haunted by Bad Rabbit. It seemed to get the greatest pleasure in setting up slip zones or small elements for the gymnasts which would not work as they should. This often resulted in broken arms or legs, or even a smashed skull one time. Patsy had felt sorry for that girl. She had been nice and offered Patsy some extra tips on how to improve her movements. The girl had a sweet smile and was so patient.

Returning to the present, Patsy grabbed the toaster from the kitchen counter. She flung it down to the soaking wet ground where instantly it sparked and flashed as electricity thrummed through it and reacted with the water. Bad Rabbit howled as he lit up like a light bulb and spasmed uncontrollably. The coffee machine went next, along with the microwave and the kettle. Finally a large glass decanter which Patsy had found and taking a liking to caught her attention. Bad Rabbit was half-crouched on the floor, its body spasming and occasionally becoming transparent enough to show its skeleton. Idly Patsy noted that the Bad Rabbit's skeleton was remarkably smaller than it should have been, but Patsy pushed the thought away as she reached up as far as she possibly could as she stood on the counter with the decanter held high above her head.

The satisfying smash as the heavy glass landed slap bang on the top of Bad Rabbit's head filled a missing hole in Patsy's heart for a second before the thump of the collection of rags that was Bad Rabbit filled the silence.

Patsy did not stick around to see the state of the creature, quickly leaping back down off the counter and to the top of the basement stairs. Desperately she slammed the door shut. Locking it, then deadbolting it down. She had installed the deadbolt to make a sort of panic room. It was a place she could hide when nosy people came looking and, not for the first time, she was more than happy that it was there. Still, she hurried down the stairs, across the small, nearly empty space and ripped open the wall-mounted cupboard that contained her shotgun.

She was in the process of loading it with shells when there was the slightest crunch of a footstep on gravel. Instantly, she was standing up, shotgun locked and loaded. Her eyes widened in surprise and confusion as standing before her was not Bad Rabbit as she had expected.

The figure was draped in a long, black, flowing hooded cape that covered a floor-length, black dress. The dress was adorned with strange looking symbols that reminded Patsy faintly of some ancient type of writing. However, the thread was such a deep, dark silver that it was next to impossible to make them out against the black fabric. No face was visible, just a white mask that resembled a cat, looking completely pristine and hauntingly beautiful. Grey swirls existed behind the slots for the eyes which betrayed no outward emotion, but Patsy knew that she was being smirked at by this creature of darkness.

Instinctively Patsy swung the shotgun up to aim at the mysterious figure. "Go to Hell with your master," she snapped towards The Collector and pulled the trigger on the shotgun.

Only for there to suddenly be no trigger beneath her finger, no gun in her hands and no longer being in the basement of her house. Once again, she was on the long winding grey and black gravel path with the gnarled trees that reached across the skyline like cruel fingers that were slowly closing in all around her to capture her and lock her down.

This time however, the sky was a chocolate-cosmos red. No stars hung there either. The wind blew too warm, filled with small, little, grey specks that brushed against Patsy's face and arms as she stared at the figure.

The Collector seemed to consider her for a moment. "Are you done playing pretend now?"

"I can break you again," Patsy threatened, though the conviction was not quite in her voice anymore. "You don't know what I'm capable of."

"Oh, I know very well what you are capable of," the Collector responded, taking a step towards Patsy that had the young woman scrambling backwards. Desperately Patsy looked for some kind of weapon but the strange, ghost-like being just kept on walking past her. "I just fail to see how you refuse to see the truth."

Patsy growled and leapt up, chasing after the figure who was always just a few steps ahead. "You're just like all those others. Never believing me! I'm a good girl! I am!"

"Hmm, we shall see," the Collector responded, turning a corner at an almost leisurely pace whilst Patsy practically sped around it. She should have collided with the Collector who was standing in her way but instead she stumbled forward another few paces and came up against nothing. Frustrated, she righted herself with every intention of screaming at this entity that had suddenly turned up in her life to cause just as many problems as Bad Rabbit did without causing the deaths of so many others.

However, her voice caught in her throat as all the colour drained away from her face. In the middle of the road, looking scorched, scratched up and battered was a large, plain cardboard box. On the top right hand corner was the white triangle symbol which Patsy had come to automatically associated with pain, tears, and fear.

The Collector was standing right next to it, never once blinking those strange, grey eyes. She remained perfectly calm and serene. The figure tilted her head to the side as she moved around the box, looking at it from multiple angles. "I wonder how this box got so damaged?" she asked aloud.

"Bad Rabbit did it," Patsy stated immediately.

"But Bad Rabbit is not here," the Collector prompted, turning her attention directly to look at Patsy. A chilling feeling passed through the girl as she stared into those swirling grey masses as if her very soul was being read and weighed up right now. "There is only you and me, Patsy. Yet this box is damaged and not another soul has been here."

Patsy was about to argue that she had just been with Bad Rabbit who had insisted on chasing her down the whole entirety of her life for no reason. However, the Collector continued before she could speak, "Have you ever actually opened this box, Patsy? Or did you allow someone else to do it?"

"What does that mean?" Patsy snapped.

"You claim that Bad Rabbit came from this box," the Collector continued, "but you never opened it yourself to confirm that. Why don't you?"

Patsy stared at the figure in disbelief. "You want me to open it?"

"I asked you why you don't open it," the Collector responded, levelly.

Patsy snarled and went to throw a punch at the Collector who merely stepped out of the way as if she were nothing more than a simple nuisance. This got the young woman riled up even more. "Why don't you stand still and let me hit you?"

"Why would anyone in their right mind allow something like that?" The Collector retorted, her voice still that same calm, almost monotone style that only held little inflections that were really starting to grate on Patsy's nerves. "Why would anyone ever allow you to hurt them, Patsy?"

"I've never hurt anyone!" Patsy shrieked, taking the bait, and charging once again at the Collector, "Why does no one ever believe me? It's always Bad Rabbit who causes everything, always Bad Rabbit that hurts, kills and destroys in its wicked and vile ways. I've begged it so many times to stop, attempted so many ways to banish it from my life and every damn time it comes back to haunt me and take away everything."

She paused to take a deep breath. "I did nothing to deserve the treatment it gives me and every time I tell people about it, they all just think I'm lying or playing pretend but good girls don't ever pretend even when everyone else around them constantly lies. They constantly make up stories to make themselves look good when they are nothing more than cheats, thieves and bastards who won't give me what I want."

"All I wanted was a nice place to call my own, parents who loved me, friends who would play with me whenever I wanted them to," Patsy continued. "But no, they had their rules, how I had to behave, how I couldn't play what I wanted because it was dangerous or could get someone hurt. Yet they'd play in that stupid park with the high climbing frames with Bad Rabbit and then whine like little brats when they got pushed off the top and broke their legs."

She stomped her foot to the ground. "I got the blame, like I had gone and done it all. I always told them that it was Bad Rabbit, that I was at home with a book and nowhere near them when it happened! But nobody ever believed me. Even when this accursed box would turn up on the doorstep after it had been thrown out, my idiotic parents would still open it up each time and there would be Bad Rabbit back in our lives, causing hell and I got the blame."

Patsy started mimicking the voices that she heard in her head. "Patsy you cannot play so rough! Patsy don't take the knives out of the drawer! Patsy why did you stab the boy in class after cutting off all his hair? Patsy why can't you just be a normal, good, little girl?"

Rage caused her to spit onto the ground. "Never once did those bastards ask if I was okay, if I was happy or if I needed help. They just allowed those other sickos to take me to councillors who treated me like I was the bad one. They treated me like I had done things that weren't supposed to be done, and I'd warn them each and every time about Bad Rabbit! But just like everyone else they didn't believe me."

She whirled around to face the Collector. "Just like right now, you've seen Bad Rabbit, you were killed by Bad Rabbit and yet you still claim that Bad Rabbit isn't real!"

The Collector stared silently at Patsy for a few seconds. "Who killed me?"

"Bad Rabbit did!" Patsy shrieked. "Picked up a rock and smashed it straight into that pretty mask to make it break! You crumpled to the ground with nothing left to hold you up bitch!"

Another beat of silence followed. "Bad Rabbit came after me." The Collector's voice was still level as she spoke.

"No, he didn't! It killed you and then started to chase me," Patsy stated in the sassiest tone that she could muster.

The Collector inclined her head forward just a little. "You're playing pretend again Patsy."

"I. Am. Not!" Patsy emphasised each word with a stomp of her foot, eyes blazing with anger.

"You are," the Collector stated in her same even tone which had not changed once during their encounter. "You're making up stories to hide your actions."

Patsy snarled. "I'll prove it to you then! Make you regret ever having doubted me!"

"How?" the Collector asked, moving back so that she was standing at what was presumably her full height. Patsy was momentarily confused as the Collector only seemed to reach five foot five, at a guess. Patsy had assumed she would have been taller. Especially given that she also seemed not to be human, if she claimed to have been killed by Bad Rabbit and yet stood before Patsy unscathed. If she was going to prove her innocence to this thing, then she was going to have to do the one thing that would unequivocally demonstrate that Bad Rabbit existed.

Without uttering a word, Patsy turned towards the battered, burnt, and splattered box in the road just a few steps away from her. Terror spiked through her heart, at the notion that she was going to willingly let Bad Rabbit out for the first time ever and she wondered vaguely what would happen. She had never allowed herself to unleash Bad Rabbit because she knew what it could do. It was always someone else who was stupid enough to open the box and release the dangerous monster that lurked underneath the lid. Maybe she could tell it to finally go away and leave her alone, or threaten to seal Bad Rabbit away in the box forever unless it started to do good things for her.

Taking a deep breath, she grabbed the lid of the box and hauled it off before heaving it out of the way as if it weighed a ton rather than the weight of a cardboard box. A stray gust of wind took hold of the flimsy material, that had seemed so heavy to Patsy, and sent it spiralling up into the air, but she did not pay the least bit of attention.

Instead she pointed an accusing finger straight into the contents of the box. "There's your proof! There's Bad Rabbit!

The Collector remained still for a very long time, as if she were waiting for something to happen. Nothing did. "Are you sure about that?" came the question in the same monotone as it had been before.

"Yes! You can see it right there!" Patsy screeched, repeatedly jabbing her finger towards the box with a look of annoyance and anger crossing her face. "Are you blind or something? It's sitting right there."

Again there was a pause, before the Collector spoke. "Have you ever looked inside that box, Patsy?"

"I don't need to look!" Patsy was shouting now, her anger boiling over. "I know it's there and I know you can see him and you're just pretending not to because you don't want to believe me!"

The Collector took a step forward. "If it is there, why has it not come out yet to attack me?"

For a second Patsy wanted to holler some more at this stupid entity who clearly had no idea how the real world worked given that it had probably been trapped in this place of 'in-between' for far too long. However, as Patsy momentarily considered the question, she became curious. Bad Rabbit was always quick to attack, regardless of friend or foe when released from the box so it was very unusual that it would choose not to do so.

Patsy snapped her gaze from the Collector to the box, following the line of her pointed finger. She frowned when she realised the box was completely empty. "Huh?" she stated, dropping her hand and stepping closer to the edge of the box to peer inside. Bad Rabbit could turn invisible, unseen by anyone but her, which made Patsy fully expect something to jump out at any second. However, nothing happened and the box was indeed completely empty. She leaned over the edge, reaching out a hand to brush over every side, every corner and flap in complete confusion. "Bad Rabbit?" she called out, wondering where it had gone this time. It always came back no matter what. It was unnerving that this time there was no sign of it.

A sudden terrifying thought filtered into her mind and she straightened up, glancing around to find no one but herself and the mysterious Collector, who was watching her. Patsy frowned at the figure. "Where is Bad Rabbit?"

Reaching forward a skeletal hand which turned into a single pointed finger, the Collector simply said, "Right here."

The bony finger touched Patsy's heart and she let out a loud shriek that could have been a mixture of denial and abject terror, but it mattered for naught. The next second she was hoisted in the air by the Collector, who was lifting Patsy with a grip that couldn't be broken by any mortal hands. "You have always denied your true nature, hidden behind your make-believe world and never once acknowledged the truth of your situation." The Collector's tone was cold, methodical and that of a judge passing sentence.

"Patsy, you are Bad Rabbit and Bad Rabbit is you," the Collector stated.

"Nooooooooooooo!" Patsy screamed before suddenly falling silent when there came the sounds of wails from all around. Twisting in the Collector's icy grip to look, Patsy saw whisp-like visions of a variety of adults and children, all looking lost, terrified, and pleading with her in a constant wail that she couldn't quite identify. Then out of the throng came a small figure, dressed in a white bunny outfit with an axe trailing along behind it and half of its face missing.

The little rabbit stopped at the feet of the Collector and tilted its head up towards Patsy. "Ma Ma?"

Finding herself dropped to the ground, Patsy stared at the thing and felt everything click into place.

Kneeling before the child, she took its disfigured head into her hands and stared at it. "You weren't going to be allowed to grow up like me," she stated, her voice utterly shattered and destroyed. "There's only room for one Bad Rabbit in this world... and that's me."

With a quick movement, she snapped the thing's neck and watched as it disappeared into the ether all around them. The skeletal hand latched back onto her throat, hauling her along the ground as Patsy shrieked and squirmed, trying to hit, bite or kick out. The Collector never once faltered in her grip.

Patsy found herself slammed into the side of a stone box, temporarily dropped to the floor as her head spun. She tried to stand up in vain, taking a swipe at the Collector who turned to her with pure, red eyes staring straight into her soul.

"Your name was marked for collection," the Collector snarled. "Your soul will rot for eternity in the very hell you made for it."

Patsy managed to scream once before she was shoved into the stone box and the lid fixed atop of it. The Collector sealed it with a single swipe of her hand and then stalked away from the many red lines that formed a familiar pentagram which glowed brightly for a few seconds before the box fell straight down into the depths of Hell.

The Collector did not bother to turn around, making her way out of the realm in between into the noise of the mortal world and walked into a figure who was standing by the exit of an alleyway.

The man was tall, with long, sand-white hair that came all the way down to the floor and wearing fine religious regalia, seemingly from an ancient civilisation. He swivelled his white ears towards her, cloak hood down as rain gently fell from the sky. "Anger only leads to misjudgement, Elzezbelle."

"Do not call me that name now," the Collector snapped. Her voice was sharp as a whip whilst her burning eyes bore holes into the street opposite. "I collected that soul and released those who were trapped by that insufferable creature. I am allowed to hate my task sometimes, Nexus."

The cat-man nodded his head. "But you are not allowed to hate yourself and you know that."

"Leave me be," the Collector responded as her hands clenched into fists. "I do not wish to be reminded of anything right now."

Nexus bowed his head and raised his hood before turning and leaving the entity in the alleyway as requested.

The Collector seethed, hissing like a riled-up cat with no way to release her pent-up frustration before suddenly looking up. Across the street, standing in the middle of the pavement was a proud looking male. A dark red hooded cloak covered his head and shoulders for the most part whilst heavy red and black fur covered his legs. A mask of a dog covered his face but piercing, red eyes faded to a beautiful pink the longer they stared at one another.

How long they stood there, merely watching one another, was impossible to say but eventually the Collector allowed something of a sigh to escape her before she turned away and faded into the blackness. Faintly she thought she heard a call of her name, but she would not answer it. There was still so much more for her to do.

Idly her fingers ran along a desk that appeared before her, caressing a glass jar which contained a skull floating in an iridescent liquid before landing on a thick, black, leather-bound book. She gathered it up, opened it and observed the name before snapping it closed and willing herself to the next task. She barely stopped to

admire the new candle that lit itself, in the room of endless candles.

Sarah was born and raised in the North East of England.

She started writing at the age of ten, when diagnosed with dyslexia initially as a way to practice her spelling and sentence structure. It turned into an life long passion and there is still far more to write.

Currently she has a full time job in the outdoor activities industry and enjoys exploring, writing, reading and crafting.

Whilst she cannot explain exactly where The Collector and The Beast came from, she can tell you the moment that they walked into her creative lives. One day, whilst on holiday in Tenerife, sitting by the swimming pool with the sun shining, the water reflecting and a nice ice drink right next to her, a vision of a room filled with endless candles appeared, followed by the desk, the book and the Collector saying 'Your name is marked, I am here to Collect'.

There will be more of the Collector and the Beast, so do keep your eyes peeled for them.